I HAD THAT SAME DREAM AGAIN

© Yoru Sumino 2016
All rights reserved.

Cover art by loundraw (FLAT STUDIO)

First published in Japan in 2016 by Futabasha Publishers Ltd., Tokyo.
English version published by Seven Seas Entertainment
under license from Futabasha Publishers Ltd.

Seven Seas press and purchase enquiries can be sent to
Marketing Manager Lianne Sentar at press@gomanga.com.
Information requiring the distribution and purchase of
digital editions is available from Digital Manager CK Russell
at digital@gomanga.com.

Seven Seas and the Seven Seas logo are trademarks of
Seven Seas Entertainment. All rights reserved.

Follow Seven Seas Entertainment online at
sevenseasentertainment.com.

TRANSLATION: Diana Taylor
ADAPTATION: Cae Hawksmoor
COVER DESIGN: KC Fabellon
INTERIOR LAYOUT & DESIGN: Clay Gardner
PROOFREADER: Dayna Abel, Brian Kearney
LIGHT NOVEL EDITOR: Nibedita Sen
PREPRESS TECHNICIAN: Rhiannon Rasmussen-Silverstein
PRODUCTION MANAGER: Lissa Pattillo
MANAGING EDITOR: Julie Davis
ASSOCIATE PUBLISHER: Adam Arnold
PUBLISHER: Jason DeAngelis

ISBN: 978-1-64505-439-9
Printed in Canada
First Printing: May 2020
10 9 8 7 6 5 4 3 2 1

I had that same Dream again

WRITTEN BY

Yoru Sumino

TRANSLATION BY

Diana Taylor

Seven Seas Entertainment

Table of Contents

Chapter 1

"**S**ENSEI, MY HEAD FEELS WEIRD. Can I skip P.E. today?" I asked, diligently raising my little elementary-schooler hand.

And yet, not only was I ordered to the faculty room after school, I was *still* made to run in the yard. I, Koyanagi Nanoka, could not accept this. I was certain I'd been called to the faculty room to be reprimanded, but I faced down my teacher without shame.

"So," I said. "I think you assumed I was just playing around earlier, asking to be let out of P.E., but I've made my own calculations and I'm pretty confident about this."

"And just what do you mean by that? Confident about what?" Hitomi-sensei asked warmly from the chair across from me. Her eyes were locked with mine and her arms folded.

My short arms folded with equal resolve. "There was a show on television last night," I told her. "Where a bunch of people were giving their opinions about an incident somewhere. There was an important-seeming person, who said that the Japanese don't like people who are weird in the head, so they run away from them. When I asked my mother who that person was, she said they were a university professor. If a university professor says so, then an elementary-schooler should accept it's true. High school is below university, and junior high is below high school, and elementary school is below them all."

My chest swelled with pride as I presented my thesis, expecting my teacher to be impressed. Instead, she looked a bit troubled, and breathed a deeper sigh than usual.

"What's the matter?" I asked.

"Well, Koyanagi-san, I do think it's wonderful that you were able to think up such a thing and express it so clearly—it means that you are very smart."

"I think so, too."

"It's also wonderful that you have such confidence. However, I have a few pieces of advice, if you would like that brilliance of yours to blossom. Will you listen?"

"Yes, of course."

Hitomi-sensei grinned and held up her index finger. "Okay. First, while it's important to try things out once you think of them, it's equally important to take a few moments to think about it before you do. Do you understand?"

I nodded my head up and down. Hitomi-sensei held up her middle finger beside the first.

"Second, running away from the things that frighten us isn't always a good thing. There are times when it's okay to run away, but exercise is important for your health, and you're already starting to sprint more quickly than you could before, aren't you?"

She was right, I *had* been able to sprint a bit more quickly today than before, but my legs were exhausted now. Could this really be good for my health?

She held up her ring finger.

"And third, I don't think what that professor said is accurate. The things that people say on TV are not necessarily always correct. You need to decide for yourself whether what you hear is true."

"In that case, Sensei..."

"Yes?"

"That also means that I have no idea whether what you're saying is correct either, doesn't it?"

She gave me a warm look. "That's right. And that is why you have to think. That said, please at least believe this: From the bottom of my heart, I wish for nothing more than your happiness, and to see you get along with others. Do you understand?"

She gave me a serious look, which I had seen many times before. I liked this expression on her. Compared to the other teachers, I felt like her face rarely lied.

I thought long and hard about what she had just said, and after careful consideration, I answered with a polite nod. "I understand. I believe you more than that professor."

"Good. In that case, from now on, before you decide to try something out in class, come discuss it with me first."

"Only if I think that's the correct thing to do."

"Yes, that's fine."

She smiled earnestly and patted me on the head. Seeing that face, I was certain that she truly did wish for my happiness. At the same time, I wondered...

"What does 'happiness' mean, according to you, Hitomi-sensei?"

"Hmm, it can mean a lot of things, but... Well, okay. I'll go ahead and tell you now. Starting in tomorrow's language arts class, we're going to be thinking about what it means to be 'happy.'"

"What? That sounds really hard."

"Yes, it's incredibly hard, but you and I and everyone else will all be thinking about what happiness means to us, personally. So try thinking about what happiness looks like to you, Koyanagi-san."

"Okay, I'll think about it."

"Very good. Keep this a secret from everyone else, okay?"

She put her finger to her lips and gave me a clumsy wink. Then, she took a piece of chocolate from Shintarou-sensei's desk, beside her.

"The first part of *my* happiness is sweets," she said.

"That might make me happy, too." I looked at Shintarou-sensei.

"Don't tell anyone about this," he said with a clumsy wink of his own. He handed me a piece of chocolate.

"I'll see you later then, Sensei," I said, waving from the doorway of the faculty room.

"Take care, then. Come to think of it, who do you usually go home with?"

"I may be a child, but I can at least make it back home on my own."

"That's true. I held you back today, but starting tomorrow, why don't you try going home with everyone else? It will be fun."

"I'll think about it. But you know, Sensei..." I put the piece of chocolate in my mouth. "Life is like a wonderful movie."

Hitomi-sensei tilted her head slightly, amused. I often said those sorts of things to her, but she always took the time to consider them. However, her conclusions were usually off the mark.

"Hmm, does that mean you're the main character?"

"Nope."

"Really? Okay, I give up. What does it mean?"

"It means that as long as you have candy, you can enjoy it even if you're alone."

Hitomi-sensei made the same troubled face as always, and I turned my back on her, hurrying home from my dreary elementary school.

There was no one home, so after putting my backpack in my room, I decided to head right back out. I made sure to lock the apartment, then took the elevator from the eleventh floor down to the first, waited for the automatic doors to open, and headed outside.

As I walked through the glass doors, I saw a friend walking nearby. She always took the opportunity to loiter around our building about the time I headed home from school. Our building was a great deal larger than the surrounding structures, so it was easy enough to find, even for her.

I offered her a greeting.

"Salutations!"

Although she knew I was there, she made a face as though she had just noticed me.

"Meow!"

"You'll never become an actress with that kind of blatant performance."

"Meow."

As always, she walked in exactly the direction I was intending, her cropped tail bobbing to-and-fro. Even my tiny footsteps outpaced her, and I was quickly able to catch up. I gave a haughty laugh, gloating over my victory, and she whipped her head away. Honestly, what a charmless girl.

As we walked toward our destination, I told my little friend about what had happened today. "It was really ridiculous!"

"Meow."

"There are some serious incompatibilities in different people's ways of thinking. Is it the same in the cat world?"

"Meow."

"That's true. It's difficult for different creatures to fully understand each other."

"Meow," she said again, disinterested.

She never seemed very engaged with what I had to say. My daily worries probably had no relevance to a cat, but it was a bit rude.

Still, there was nothing I could do about it, so I decided to sing a song. Something that she could enjoy as well. The only two things that drew the attention of my cheeky little friend were milk and the sound of my song. What a luxurious life she led.

I began to sing my favorite tune. "Happiness won't cooome wandering my way sooo..."

"Meow meow!"

"Thaaaaat's why I set ouuut to find it todaaay!"

Although she pretended not to be interested, the tone of her meowing was more inflected than usual. She had such a lovely singing voice. Although she was never forthcoming, I'm sure she had all the boy cats flocking to her with a beautiful voice like that.

As the two of us walked along the quiet road, singing together, the path dead-ended at the banks of a wide river. We climbed the stairs up the embankment. There were no large buildings around, and the wind was forceful. It felt wonderful blowing through my hair. The next town over sat on the opposite bank, and I smelled something slightly foreign.

This embankment was a popular place for children to play, but I had no interest in that. Miss Bobtail showed some interest in a ball rolling along the embankment, but there was no ball that interested her more than a bowl of cream.

We continued along the path beside the river, singing. As we walked, we greeted those we passed. We walked by the old man sitting on some cardboard, and an old woman whom we saw often down at the shopping arcade gave me candy. Eventually, our destination came into view: a cream-colored two-story apartment building. It sat in front of us like a large square buttercream cake. We descended the stairs down from the embankment and approached it.

We trotted into the apartment, Miss Bobtail being careful not to make too much noise. Climbing the stairs a step ahead of me, she mewled at the apartment door at the end of the second floor. I had told her to be quiet, but she was often quick to forget things like that. She was not as clever as me.

I strode elegantly up to the door and pushed the button that Miss Bobtail was not tall enough to reach. A few seconds later, I heard the doorbell ringing within. Before I could even spot the ant crawling over my foot, the door opened.

Inside stood a lovely young woman wearing a T-shirt and long trousers, as she always did. Her hair was a bit more unkempt, and she seemed more tired than usual.

"Hello!" I said.

"Hello there. You're in good spirits today, little miss."

"Yes, I'm doing well. Are you not feeling well today, Skank-san?"

"No, I'm fine. I just only woke up."

"But it's already after three o'clock!"

"There are some people for whom three o'clock is the morning. I'm one of them."

"Are there others?"

"Americans, anyway."

I began to giggle at the absurdity of her casual reply. Perhaps following my lead, she began to laugh too, scratching at her neck.

"C'mon in," she said. "I'm sure Miss Kitty is hungry, too."

I shed my shoes and entered Skank-san's home, but Miss Bobtail lingered outside. What a wicked girl she was, to only behave herself at a time like this.

Skank-san poured some milk into an old dish and took it out-side to offer it to my friend, then shut the door and handed me a bottle of Yakult. I sipped the drink, and watched as Skank-san fixed her bedhead.

I usually came here to play on school days. Skank-san was an adult, which meant she was busy, and there were plenty of times that she was not here when I arrived. But when she was here, she always gave me a Yakult, and sometimes some ice cream. Miss Bobtail knew of Skank-san's kindness as well, and so always followed me, looking forward to her saucer of milk.

Skank-san opened the window and took a sandwich from the fridge, then sat down upon her unmade bed. I took a place at the round table in the center of the room, savoring my Yakult.

"So how was school today, little miss?"

The light from the window shone through her long hair as she munched her egg sandwich, giving her an angelic glow. I ex-plained to Skank-san what I had told to Miss Bobtail earlier. She listened, nodding along silently, until I said "I had a good idea, but nothing to back it up with."

She laughed loudly. "I'm sure no one thinks that you're crazy."

"Why's that?"

"Because you're smart. When you're smart, even if you act a little strange, people just assume you're thinking about something. That's why you were called to the faculty room, right?"

"That's true. In that case, next time I'll try to make an even stranger face."

I stuck out my tongue and she laughed loudly again.

"Sounds like you have a good teacher."

"That's true, she's a really good teacher. Even if she's kind of off the mark sometimes."

"All adults tend to be off the mark," she said, standing to take a can out from the fridge.

"Is that sweet?" I asked.

"It's sweet, but bitter, too."

"But why would you wanna drink something that's bitter? You drink coffee too, don't you? That's even more bitter. Are you punishing yourself?"

"No, I'm drinking it because I like it. I drink both alcohol and coffee. I didn't drink coffee when I was a child, though. Adults are the only ones who enjoy bitter things."

"I see. Then I wonder if I'll think bitter things are tasty someday, too."

"You just might. But, there's no reason to force yourself to drink them. I think it's wonderful to only be able to enjoy sweet things," she said with a glimmering smile.

There was a wonderful smell around her. Not like perfume, and not like other adults. When I told her that once, she laughed and said: "That's because I'm not a proper adult."

If that was true, then I never wanted to be a proper adult, either.

"Life is like a crème brûlée," I said.

"How do you mean?"

"The sweet parts are the only good parts, but there are people who enjoy the bitter parts, too."

"Aha ha, that's very true." Skank-san gulped her drink with a smile. "You really are smart, little lady."

I was thrilled to hear such praise.

"Skank-san, has anything interesting happened at your work?"

"There's nothing interesting at my work."

"Really? But my mother and father love their jobs. They're never at home."

"Just because they're always working doesn't mean their jobs are fun, though it is wonderful if they do something interesting."

"I'm sure it's fun for them. Even more fun than playing with me."

"If you're lonely, then you should speak up and tell them."

I shook my head. "That's not a very clever thing to say." Then I asked something that had been bothering me. "If you don't like your job, then does that mean you aren't happy?"

She did not answer. Instead, she laughed thinly. "I think what makes me happiest right now is seeing you."

I was thrilled about that. It wasn't the sort of lie that adults told to disguise the truth.

"Happiness won't cooome wandering my way sooo, thaaat's why I set ooout to find it todaaay!"

"I love that song, too. 'Take one step a day and you'll keep going on your way!'"

"It's three steps forwaaard, and two steps back!" we sang together.

"I'm supposed to be thinking about what happiness is," I told her. "We'll be talking about it in class."

"Huh, we did something like that when I was little, too. That really takes me back. What do you think happiness is for you, little miss?"

"I still don't know. I've just started thinking about it."

"That's a difficult problem. How about some ice cream, to give you just a little hint?"

"I'll have some!"

We played a game of Othello together, as we always did—each of us munching on a soda-flavored ice lolly. Skank-san had owned the Othello set since childhood. My father had bought me a set too, but there was no one at home for me to play with. Still, it comforted me to know that when Skank-san stopped by my house, we would be able to play there, too. As to which of us was the stronger player, well, one day I would be able to show her it was me.

When I finally took a victory, after she had already won twice, she looked to the clock on the wall.

"Oh, it's already four o'clock."

As I thought about how quickly the time had passed, we cleaned up the Othello set.

"Thank you for the Yakult and the ice cream, Skank-san."

"No, thank you for coming."

I always left Skank-san's home around four. I would have loved to stay longer, to talk and play some more Othello, but I had other destinations to visit.

I donned my pink shoes, which fitted my little feet perfectly, gave my thanks again to Skank-san, and opened the door. Outside, the Miss Bobtail sat politely, having finished her milk. Skank-san picked up the empty dish.

"I'll see you next time," I said.

"Of course, come by anytime you like," she replied.

"What are your plans for the rest of the day, Skank-san?"

"I think I might sleep a bit. To get ready for work."

"Good luck with your work. Take care of yourself."

"Will do. And good luck with finding your happiness. If you find it along your walk, make sure you come back and tell me."

"Okay. Good night, then."

Skank-san waved, and I shut the door. She had a strange job, one that started after I went to bed and finished before I woke up. I did not know the details, but I could not work like she did, staying up all night and sleeping all day, so for that alone she had my utmost respect.

I thought about her job as Miss Bobtail and I descended the stairs. In the past, when I'd asked about her job, she laughed and said: "I attend a midnight court."

I was sure that must be the most wonderful job.

It had been on a cold and rainy day some time ago that I'd first met Bobtail and Skank-san. I'd donned my cute pink boots, brought out my pretty red umbrella, and been walking along the embankment in my fluttering yellow poncho, chasing a little frog. The little green frog was so pretty, and it quite dutifully made its way down the middle of the sidewalk, so I could keep following.

Somewhere along the way, I began jumping too. I laughed to myself, imagining that the two of us were doing some sort of special training together. The frog put all it had into that training. Surely it was a shy little thing, only conducting its training on rainy days, when there were few people around. I cheered the stalwart little frog on.

But perhaps the frog didn't hear this encouragement, or perhaps it simply wasn't planning to train today, because eventually it hopped off, scampered into the grass, and vanished. I was sad to see it go, but although I waded into the grass myself, and no matter how much I muddied my boots, I could not find the frog again.

I was filled with a sense of gloom, but there was nothing I could do. By now, I had pushed my way all the way to the riverside. I decided to climb back up the embankment, but I proceeded along a different path, never abandoning the hope that perhaps fate would help me find the frog again.

A bobtail cat was waiting for me at the end of the path, huddled in the grass. I ran over to her, kicking my way through puddles. She was covered in mud, flecked with red here and there. More than anything, I noticed that her tail was only half as long as it should be.

How terrible, I thought.

I did not wonder who she was, nor how she had ended up this way. I folded my umbrella and gently wrapped her up my arms, carrying her up the bank so as not to startle her. I could sense her quiet breathing.

At first, I thought I might take her back home. However, I quickly discarded that idea when I realized there would be no one else there. I couldn't mend her wounds alone.

My face was cold from the rain, and I was sure that she must be cold too. I thought about whom I could implore for help. I climbed down the bank opposite the river and ran to the nearby cream-colored apartment building. Although I ran a bit recklessly, the cat did not stir in my arms.

I rang doorbells on the building's first floor, starting from the end. There was no reply at the first door, nor was there one at the next, or the next, or the next. Finally, the fifth door swung open, but the woman who answered closed it again the moment she laid eyes on me. I kept trying at door after door, but there was no one home at most of them, and when occasionally someone *did* open the door, no one was interested in hearing me out. The little one in my arms was trembling.

I reached the last door of the building. My heart was racing as I pressed the doorbell. Her gentle breathing was growing fainter, and I was afraid that she might be fading away in my arms. I heard the bell ring within, then other sounds. At first, I was relieved to know that there was someone inside. There were plenty of other doors where there was no one present, even if the lights were on.

Footsteps approached slowly, someone unfastened the lock, and the knob turned. The moment that the door opened, I shouted: "Please save her!"

The beautiful woman looked at me in shock for a few moments. She looked at the little one in my arms. I stared into her eyes. *You must look people in the eyes when you're speaking to them*, Hitomi-sensei had told me.

The young woman's eyes stopped on my new friend's trembling form, and then she did something that no one had done: she looked back into my eyes.

"Just a minute."

She stepped inside, and returned with a towel. She took the little soul from my arms and took her inside, wrapping her up.

"You come in, too. Take off your coat and shoes."

Hearing her gentle voice, I felt such relief I could have fallen asleep right then and there, but I needed to thank her first. I wondered what her name could be, and my eyes fell on the nameplate fixed beside the door.

I read the letters that were crudely scrawled over the nameplate in black magic marker.

"Skank...?"

It was a strange name. It didn't sound Japanese at all. I wondered if she might be a foreigner, though she didn't look it. I tilted my head curiously.

"Come on now, come inside, I'm not scary."

The woman insisted that I have a bath before thanking her, and before I knew it I was washing myself. When I stepped out of the bathroom, some adult-sized pajamas were set out for me in place of my soaked clothes, and I gratefully slipped into them. The woman was wrapping the little cat in bandages. I watched her hands as she worked, not wishing to get in the way.

"Thank you, really," I said, when she had finally finished her doctoring.

"No problem. I put your clothes in the dryer, so you can wait here until they're ready."

"Okay. Um...Skank-san?"

She looked taken aback when I said her name. Perhaps she was surprised that I knew it.

"That was what it said on your nameplate out front," I explained. "It's okay if I call you Skank-san, right?"

"You mean as my name?"

"Yes."

As I nodded, she let out a great laugh. I hadn't the slightest clue what that was supposed to mean. However, I was glad that she seemed to be amused, so I started to laugh, too.

"Aha ha. Ah, yeah, that's just fine. That's my name."

"Are you from another country?"

"No, I'm Japanese."

"Huh, that's a weird name."

Skank-san laughed again.

"Skank-san?" I said. "I can rewrite your nameplate for you, as a thank you for saving this little one. It might be rude, but I can't say those letters are very well-written. My handwriting is much better."

But she just shook her head. "Mm, I appreciate the offer, but it's not the sort of thing I'd want you to bother with. I didn't write it there, either."

"Huh? So who wrote it?"

This time, she laughed thinly. "I've already forgotten who it was."

And so I became friends with Skank-san and Miss Bobtail. Hitomi-sensei seemed to think that I didn't have any friends, but in fact, I had wonderful friends. Friends who would play Othello with me. Who would walk with me. And I had friends who would talk to me about books.

That was why, even if I had no friends at school, and even if my father and mother were too busy to ever play with me, I was not lonely.

My first meeting with Granny was not as fraught as the day I met Skank-san and Miss Bobtail. When I say it was not fraught, I mean that I was not sad or in pain at the time.

If you climbed the hills through the trees near my home, you would find a clearing, and there in that clearing was a wooden house. One day, I came upon this house, and spent a long time looking at it, thinking how wonderful it was and how unusual for our area. After some time, I knocked on the front door, wondering if the place was abandoned. It was terribly quiet, but an old woman with a lovely smile opened the door.

From that day on, we would be friends.

Today, the spacious wooden house was as wonderful as always.

"How are the sweets you make so tasty, Granny?"

"When you've lived as long as I have, you learn how to make things taste good. That's all," Granny said nonchalantly, sipping her tea.

As I nibbled on the madeleines she had made, I tried to unravel the secret of their deliciousness. Miss Bobtail lounged in the sun flooding the plank floor corridor that ran between the living room and the open field.

"I found that book you were telling me about," I said, sitting at the low table in the tatami-floored room. "*The Little Prince*. It's in the school library, so I tried reading it."

"Did you like it?"

"Mm, I liked how it was written, but it was kind of hard."

"Was it? You really are sharp, Nacchan."

"I've thought so too, but I'm not really there yet. I didn't get it at all."

"It's important to know what you do not know. The worst thing you can do is to think that you understand something when you really don't."

"Is that how it is?"

"Even not understanding it means it left some impression on you, didn't it?"

"That's true. I think having a cat to talk with suits me better than a quiet sheep in a box."

Granny laughed softly and looked at the little one sleeping on the floor. "Such wonderful praise from you, and all she does is sleep."

"That's fine. She always does what she wants."

Miss Bobtail yawned, her tail swaying back and forth. It was contagious, and I opened my mouth in an unseemly manner to let out a yawn of my own. Then, I decided to talk to Granny about the same thing I had discussed with Skank-san—the conversation from school. When I told her the whole story from start to finish, Granny laughed out loud, just like Skank-san had.

"I see, I see. That sounds dreadful, making you run in the yard and stay after school."

"It wasn't. I mean, I hated P.E., but it wasn't so bad staying after. I do like Hitomi-sensei."

"She sounds like a wonderful teacher."

"Yeah, she is. Even if she kind of misses the mark. Hee hee, I had this same conversation with Skank-san."

"Did you win at Othello today?"

"Only one time. But even then, I still lost twice. I wonder if I'll get better at it someday."

"You will. You have the power to see the future, after all. That's an indispensable power when it comes to games."

I knew that Granny would never tell a lie, so I was thrilled to hear this. There was a wonderful smell around her, not like incense. A wonderful smell unlike other adults. When I told her that once, she smiled and said "That's because I've already graduated from being an adult."

"That means that Skank-san has the power to see the future, too," I said.

"I wonder. Unlike children, adults are usually creatures who look back into the past."

"But Skank-san is better than me."

"That's because she's lived longer, Nacchan. She knows how to win better than you."

Granny talked often about how long people had lived. But she was right, she had lived at least seven times as long as me, which was probably why her madeleines were much better.

I reached out to grab a second one, but then withdrew my hand. If I were to have two madeleines on top of the Yakult and the ice cream, I wouldn't have any room for the dinner my mother made.

I decided to use my brain for something else, to make myself forget about the madeleines.

"We have an assignment in school," I said. "To think about happiness."

"That sounds like an interesting lesson."

"It is. But it's really hard. It would be fine if we could talk about as many things as we like, but we only have as long as the class period, and I'm not the only one in the class."

"That's true. You have to put all those things in order, and pull your answer out from the middle."

"I want to find an answer that will surprise Hitomi-sensei, that everyone in my class will understand."

I felt a swelling of pride imagining Hitomi-sensei's praise. Letting myself get carried away, I started reaching for another madeleine, but I held back at the last moment. Granny saw me and laughed.

"What's your happiness, Granny?"

"My happiness, hm? Lots of things. Drinking tea on sunny days like this, and whenever you stop by this lonely home. However, thinking of a single answer would be difficult. I'll think about it."

"Yeah, think about it. Come to think of it, Granny, are you happy right now?"

Granny took a sip of tea and smiled. "Yes, I am."

She appeared that way, and the feeling spread to me as well. When I looked out to the hall, Miss Bobtail was sleeping happily as well. *This old wooden home must be filled with the essence of happiness,* I thought.

"Oh right, can you tell me another book to read?"

"You said that you already read *Tom Sawyer,* yes?"

"Yeah, it was fun."

"Well then, how about a story about Tom's good friend?"

"You mean Homeless Huck? Is there another book?"

"Oh, you hadn't heard, then? It's called *The Adventures of Huckleberry Finn.* It's a lot of fun. If it's not in the school's library, you could ask Hitomi-sensei about it."

Hearing this wonderful news, I tucked the name of the book away in the same part of my brain where I kept my most important memories.

We both loved talking about books, and so I never noticed how much time had passed.

Which was your favorite story from The Little Prince? *I liked the one about the Prince and the rose. It was so charming. What about you, Granny? The one about the snake who ate the elephant, maybe.*

As we carried on like this, an orange hue washed over the world outside. I looked at the clock on the wall to see that it was already half past five. I had to get back home by six. I promised my mother that I would.

I woke my friend with the flicking tail and said my farewells to Granny.

"I'll see you next time, Granny."

"Take care on the way home, now."

"I will. I'll look for the book about Huck, too."

I waved to Granny, who had come to the front door to see me off, and Miss Bobtail and I climbed the footpath down the hill. The path was gorgeous. Orange-colored. I was never sad to say goodbye like this. I always had tomorrow after all, and the day after that.

"Happiness won't cooome, wandering my way sooo, thaaat's why I set ooout to find it todaaay!"

"Meow meow!"

I parted ways with my bob-tailed friend and headed home to do my homework. Around half past six, my mother returned home. She was out of the house even on Saturdays and Sundays sometimes, but she was always home at dinnertime. I thought how nice it would be if it was always dinnertime, but then I would have to give up on the yogurt I had at breakfast.

Today's dinner was curry rice. Even though I'd already had Yakult and ice cream and a madeleine, I still had seconds of the rice.

"I wonder if I should go on a diet," I said.

My mother laughed. "You don't need to," she said, handing me a cookie she had gotten at work.

I couldn't help myself. I ate the cookie with vanilla ice cream on top.

"Maybe having your favorite ice cream with a cookie is happiness," I said.

"For me it's with coffee," said my mother, sitting in front of me as she dunked her cookie in her mug and ate it.

And then, as always, I took my bath and I grew tired around ten o'clock. And, as always, I did not talk to my mother, nor to my father who returned after I had gone to sleep, about my conversation with Skank-san.

Chapter 2

IF I HAD TO GIVE my mood a color as I donned my indoor shoes at the elementary school lockers, it would be grey. Mostly because of all the unpleasant people I'd run into that morning. At times like these, you'd usually say that you were feeling blue, but I liked the color blue.

"Oh man, the weirdo's here!" a voice I did not recognize called from inside.

I gave a theatrical sigh. "You all really must be stupid if you can't beat a weirdo like me on tests. How fascinating."

Gratified by the looks of anger on the faces of several of my idiot classmates, I refused to converse with them further. Eventually one of them said something like: "Why're you such a baby?"

I wanted to praise them for being able to even speak intelligibly, but they left, and so I put on my indoor shoes and went into the building.

Just then...

"Morning, Koyanagi-san."

A single voice put a halt to my grey-colored shuffling. I turned around to see one of my classmates, and my expression turned dark.

"Oh! Morning, Ogiwara-kun."

"I just finished reading *Tom Sawyer* yesterday," he said. "It was really good."

"Did you? That's great. Which scenes did you like?"

"The part about the paint, I guess. I thought Tom was really cool, too."

"Tom really is appealing. And smart."

"I liked Huck, too."

"Homeless Huck, right? Oh, come to think of it, I'm—"

I stopped. Not because I was trying to keep my talk with Granny to myself, but because a boy came running up from behind Ogiwara-kun and crashed into him. I turned my back on the startled Ogiwara, but I doubt he even saw it. The boy who had run into him was a close friend, and had most certainly run into Ogiwara in the name of boyish roughhousing, not bullying. No one would bully Ogiwara-kun, nor would he bully anyone. He had a lot of friends.

I, on the other hand, had no friends in our class and elected to turn my back on this. Other than Ogiwara, everyone else in our class either thought I was clumsy or hated me. Still, I had never once been bullied by them. And so, I decided to make my exit first, upon noticing Ogiwara's friend. A friendship between boys isn't something a girl should get in the middle of.

I needed to stop at the library before I could head to the classroom. The library opened first thing in the morning, which was wonderful for me. I much preferred to spend the raucous period before Hitomi-sensei arrived in the quiet library.

When I entered, I was greeted by the unique smell of the books and the kind librarian. I asked the librarian if they had *The Adventures of Huckleberry Finn,* which I'd heard about from Granny the day before. The librarian guided me to a bookshelf and left me to seek out the book myself.

"If you're a lover of books, you'll want to enjoy the heart-pounding feeling of searching for them," she said.

I felt the same way.

I quickly found the book in question and picked it up, my fingertips tingling with excitement. I dropped my bag and took a nearby seat.

I'm sure that Ogiwara-kun and I were the only ones in our class who understood the incomparable feeling of opening the first page of a book. It would be wasted on the others.

All alone, I took the first tiny step into the tale of Homeless Huck.

The library was a wonderful place, with its quiet, its lovely smell, and the kind librarian. However, even here, there was one line that one must not cross: losing oneself too deeply in the world of books.

Until the librarian called out, I'd completely forgotten that I was still at school. Just before the morning bell rang, the librarian called my name and, after what seemed like ages, I returned to my own world. I borrowed the book, stuffed it into my bag, and bid farewell for now.

I passed through the hallways, noisier now than when I arrived, and climbed the stairs one by one to my third-floor class-room. Ignoring the boys who ran through the hallways, I stepped inside. No one seemed to take notice of me entering the room. As always, I marched straight to my seat in the very last row. I put down my backpack and sat down.

Kiriyuu-kun, who sat beside me, noticed me and hurriedly shut the notebook on his lap.

"Good morning, Kiriyuu-kun."

"G-good-good morning, Koyanagi-san."

He was talking quickly, the way he did when he was upset at being teased. He shoved the closed notebook into his desk.

"What were you drawing?"

"N-nothing!"

He was lying. I always knew when Kiriyuu-kun was lying. He had been drawing a picture. He was always doodling in his notebook. He perhaps thought that he was doing a good job of hiding it, but I was his neighbor—I saw everything.

He was really skilled at drawing, something that I thought he ought to be crowing about to the people around him, but he never did, and the idiot boys ridiculed him again and again for it.

"Kiriyuu-kun, life is like a cavity."

"Wh-what do you mean?"

"If you don't like it, you should hurry up and do something about it. If people are making fun of you for drawing, then you should just spit it back in their faces," I said, putting my backpack onto the shelf behind me and taking my seat once more.

"I-I can't do that," Kiriyuu said quietly, not looking my way.

"Not with that weak attitude you can't," I said, just as the bell rang.

Hitomi-sensei entered the classroom. Everyone loved Hitomi-sensei—the only time the atmosphere seemed clear and bright was when she was there.

"Good morning!"

"Goood mooorniiing!"

At the direction of Ogiwara, the class representative, we began another boring day of school.

First period was math, second was social studies, and then in third period we had the lesson about happiness that Hitomi-sensei had mentioned to me. I wanted to proudly announce that I'd known about it since yesterday, but I had been sworn to secrecy. I mentioned neither the lesson nor the chocolate.

The fifty-minute class passed quickly, reading the story in our textbook and thinking about the main character's feelings. There was no time to think about happiness. Then Hitomi-sensei announced that fourth period would be an extension of the third. I very much approved of this idea, and thought that fifty minutes was not nearly enough.

In fourth period, we had to come up with various notions of happiness. We were split into pairs, and had to exchange what we thought of as our own happiness.

I was paired with my neighbor, Kiriyuu-kun. Kiriyuu was rarely one to talk unprompted, so I had to lead the conversation.

"Yesterday, I was eating a cookie with ice cream on top. I felt happy then."

"Huh."

"Did you have anything like that?"

"Well, umm, the ohagi that my grandma made were really good."

"Sweets that grandmas make are always super tasty!"

"Yeah. I like the ones my mom makes too, though. They're different from Grandma's."

"Your mom makes sweets too? That's nice. My mom doesn't get home until nighttime."

The two of us continued discussing like this, jotting things down in our notebooks. We were on task, and when Hitomi-sensei made the rounds to check in she gave us praise, but there was one thing that still bothered me. No matter how much we discussed the topic, even when I mentioned books, Kiriyuu-kun never said anything about drawing. I thought this was strange, so I asked.

"Aren't you happy when you're drawing?"

"Uh, m-maybe? I...do like it."

"Then that's one thing that makes you happy."

"B-but whenever I d-draw...people make fun of me..."

"That doesn't matter!"

My voice was louder than I intended. Kiriyuu-kun seemed shocked, but so did everyone else in the room. I was surprised at myself, too.

"Sorry, I just got excited!" I told Hitomi-sensei, who was looking my way.

"Try not to startle everyone," she replied gently, and although everyone was muttering, calm returned.

I turned back to Kiriyuu. "Stuff like that doesn't matter."

I jotted down "drawing wonderful pictures" on my page. Kiriyuu-kun hung his head, silent.

As fourth period ended and lunch subsequently wrapped up, I spent the rest of my midday break in the library. It was noisier now than it was in the morning, but it was still quieter than the classroom, and I was able to bury myself in the adventures of Homeless Huck.

After break was clean-up time, so when the bell rang, I returned to the classroom and grabbed a broom. Kiriyuu-kun, being in the same group, had also returned ahead of time to start cleaning.

As we diligently cleaned the room, that idiot boy from before returned from the gymnasium, spouting some stupid nonsense.

"You two are super creepy, always drawin' your pictures and readin' all those books."

"The only creepy thing here is your face," I replied dutifully. "Did you know that?"

I flashed a look at Kiriyuu to see if he would reply as well, but naturally he did not.

Fifth and sixth period ended. As it came time for afternoon announcements, I let out a sigh of relief, releasing all the anticipation I had been holding in. We gave our farewells to Hitomi-sensei, and then it was over...or so I thought. But there was still one important announcement for us.

"The week after next we'll be having a class visit. All of your mothers and fathers have already been informed about this, but this will be an important chance for them to see what you're normally like at school, so make sure you give them handout I'm passing around, okay? Please promise me that, everyone."

"Yes, ma'am," we chorused, passing the handouts back from the front row.

I read the contents of the sheet, then happily slipped it into my bag. I loved these observation days. It was a chance for my mother and father to see just how clever I was.

Without being called to stay behind today, I went home alone as I usually did. I put my backpack in my room as always, and started to head back out when I remembered something important. I returned to my room and pulled out the handout, placing it on the living room table before I set out again.

Outside the building, as always, my bob-tailed friend was waiting for me.

"Meow!" she cried in greeting.

We both set out towards the great rolling river. As we climbed the bank, a breeze blew pleasantly through my hair and rippled across her short tail. Feeling wonderful, we both began to sing. Before long, our voices still ringing, we arrived at the cream-colored apartment building, where we stood at the usual door and rang the bell. The first time, we heard nothing. The door did not open the second time, either. Miss Bobtail mewled at my feet as I rang a third time, but no reply came.

"I guess she must be out today."

"Meow."

Skank-san was a busy woman, so she was frequently out of the house. Letting the wind wash away our disappointment, we gave up and decided to return by a different path. Obviously, we weren't going home yet. We had a usual appointment after Skank-san's place.

We walked along while singing, passing between houses both big and small. Soon we passed by the building where I lived, before heading along the usual path to the hills that rose behind it. I greeted the locals we passed along the way, but my standoff-ish friend merely waved her tail back and forth, coolly averting her gaze.

"Never mind just humans," I said. "You're going to end up despised in the world of cats that way."

She continued to walk ahead of me, as though she had not heard me, arriving at the foot of the hill and steadily beginning the climb through the trees. Finally we reached the usual clearing, with its house made of wood, and rushed to knock on the door.

The first time we knocked, there was no response.

We knocked several more times, tried the knob, and circled the house's perimeter, but it seemed that Granny was not home.

I sat down in the greenery of that empty space and crossed my short arms.

"It's weird for both Skank-san and Granny to be out."

"Meow meow," Miss Bobtail replied, forlorn that she had yet to receive a meal.

"Now you can't just sulk about it. Life is like a school lunch."

"Meow."

"You've still got to enjoy it as much as you can, even when they don't have the things you like. You get it?"

She did not appear to get it, but we descended the hill together anyway. *Maybe we will run into Granny on her return,* I thought, but we arrived at the park at the bottom of the hill without any such luck. In the park, children younger than me were running around, their mothers watching over them.

Now then, what could be going on? I wondered. Miss Bobtail rolled around at my feet, perhaps distraught that all her hopes had been betrayed.

I set the gears of my sharp mind turning. Then I remembered something.

"There's a fork in the road on the way to Granny's house."

"Meow."

"Now that I think about it, there's still a way we haven't gone. Let's try going that way."

Miss Bobtail was still flopped on her side on the ground. I nudged her with my toe. She stood somewhat reluctantly, let out a big yawn, and we began climbing the hill again.

I followed behind her, sweat dotting my forehead. Finally, we arrived at the fork. We always went right from here but today, for the first time, I decided to try left. This path sprawled to a gentle rise. Perhaps pepped up by the chance for some exercise, Miss Bobtail sprang along ahead of me. Cats are such easygoing creatures.

Five minutes later, with the smell of the trees growing stronger bit by bit, the broken iron gate appeared. The gate, which appeared as if by magic, was open just a few centimeters.

As I reached out to touch it, the gate swung slowly open, crying out in a hoarse voice. I hesitated for just a moment, but I looked Miss Bobtail in the eye, thinking how far we had already come, and decided to proceed. I already had plenty of practice looking up and sticking out my tongue for forgiveness, just in case anyone got mad at us.

Beyond the gate were clean-cut stone steps, unlike the rough path we had climbed. We went up carefully, but eventually the stairs ran out and opened up into something like a clearing, strewn with gravel.

I was surprised to see it, and drank in a breath of this new air. I have no idea whether the little one at my feet was surprised as well.

"Meow," she said, as she always did.

"I had no idea there was something like this up here."

At the end of the path opposite from Granny's house was something that was the complete opposite: a building that looked like a square stone box. Looking at the window-like holes along the walls, I thought the building had two stories, but I didn't have the slightest clue what it was. There were no patterns or lettering anywhere. It looked very much just like a plain stone box. It had none of the warmth of Granny's big wooden house.

As I drew closer, I found there wasn't even a door in the place where the entrance should have been. Puzzling over this for a moment, I slipped timidly in through one of the gaping holes. Miss Bobtail swallowed her nerves and casually entered the building. I entered behind her. Don't tell anyone, but I was actually a bit afraid.

First we looked around the ground level, but there were nothing resembling rooms. The floor was a solid plane, utterly empty. There was not the slightest hint that anyone might be there. The only thing even marking this box as a building was the staircase that sat smack in the middle. With nowhere else to go, we mustered our courage and slowly climbed the stairs.

The second floor was empty as well. It appeared as though the square holes really had been windows once, as there were shards of glass still hanging from them here and there. Obviously, I did not touch them—that would be dangerous.

Ah, nothing left in this building, I thought, looking around the second floor.

Don't tell anyone, but it really was frightening. I wanted nothing more than to hurry back outside. But then we discovered another set of stairs, leading up. Looking up, I could tell it led to the roof, seeing the open sky above. I locked eyes with the little one at my feet and we decided to climb.

Step by step we climbed the stairs, leaving footprints behind in the dust. When we poked our heads out onto the rooftop, I was greeted first by rays of sun, and the wind brushing my face. And then I locked eyes with a young woman sitting huddled on the ground with a box cutter pressed to her wrist.

That day, shocked to my core, I understood for the first time what people meant when they say that time stopped. And then, an instant later, time was racing.

"Waaaaaaaaaaaaaaaaaaaaaaaaaaaaaaaaaaah!!"

"Waaaaaaaaaaaaaaaaaaaaaaaaaaaahh!!!"

"Meow!"

And that was how I met Minami-san.

I had that
same
Dream
again

Chapter 3

MINAMI-SAN SCREAMED at the same time I did, while Miss Bobtail bounded happily onto the roof.

Minami-san dropped the blade onto the stone floor. After getting over my shock, I looked between Minami-san, the blade, and Minami-san's wrist, and was shocked again. Red blood dripped from her hand.

"What're you doing?! We need to fix that!"

"Wh-who are you?"

"I've got a band-aid—here, put this on and let's get you to the hospital!"

"Wait, um...I'm fine. Stop fussing, would you?"

I was panicking, but Minami-san had already calmed down. I only learned her age later, but she was very much a mature high school student.

Hearing her request, I thought of how Hitomi-sensei had taught me to calm myself down and started breathing deeply.

Breathing like this opened a gap in the tension in my heart and my nerves relaxed, as they had that time I found myself wrapped in slightly-too-large pajamas.

Deep breath in...and out.

I repeated this breathing many times finally and began to relax. I handed Minami-san a handkerchief and band-aid.

"I've got one," Minami said reluctantly, pressing her own handkerchief to her wrist. My band-aid was set down on the rooftop, unused.

I looked at Minami-san's wrist and the downturned corners of her mouth. "Is something wrong with your head?" I asked.

"Probably," she said dully through those twisted lips.

"I see... So when you *are* weird in the head, you start cutting up your own arm. That could never happen to me, then. I hate pain."

"So do I."

"But you're still cutting your arm. You really are weird."

"Shut up. Go away."

Not listening, I climbed up onto the roof. I sat down beside Minami-san and Miss Bobtail, quietly observing her wrist. I could sense Minami-san making a sour face, but I just couldn't leave an injured person alone. But looking at the painful cut, I grew frightened imagining it on myself, and turned to look at her face instead.

"What're you looking at?" she asked.

"Your arm. It looks really painful."

"You're a child. Go home already."

"What are you doing up here, Minami-san?"

"It's none of your business. And where did you get 'Minami' from?"

"Well your name's written right there, isn't it? Even an elementary schooler can read that."

I pointed to the letters embroidered on her navy blue skirt. I could only dream of wearing something so sharp and rigorous. However, Minami-san only looked at her skirt and let out a sigh.

"What's wrong?"

"I'm not doing anything."

"Are you alone?"

"It's...nice to be alone, isn't it? Nothing says you have to be with someone."

"That's true. I've had the same thought."

"You sound pretty conceited for a child."

"I'm not conceited. Well, maybe a little more than the other kids. I know how wonderful books can be."

"People hate you, don't they?"

"Probably," I said, mimicking her.

She scowled and turned to look at Miss Bobtail, who was looking back, her head tilted. She surely thought this whole thing was as strange as I did. As she could not speak, I had to be her representative.

"So, Minami-san."

"Yeah?"

"Why were you cutting your arm?"

"Why do I have to explain something like that to you when I've only just met you?"

"I don't see why not. I'm not going to spread rumors about you."

She turned her face away, still scowling, and I just assumed that I would not be getting an answer. However, at length, she finally replied.

"No reason. Helps me calm down."

"If you need to calm down, you should breathe in, open your heart, and take in the smell of the sun in an old wooden house."

"This calms me down in the same way."

"Well that sounds weird."

"You...wanna try it?"

She clicked open the box cutter, covered in dried blood, and held it out to me. I quickly shook my head. As she closed the blade, she looked like she might have been smiling, just a little. It was impossible to tell, with her eyes almost fully covered by her hair.

"What would you do if I was some kind of bad guy? It'd be easy to cut a kid like you."

"It's fine. I haven't gotten any bad smells from you."

"How's that fine?"

"You don't smell like a bad adult."

"That's because I'm not an adult."

I really was getting worried about her wrist now, and mustered the courage to reach out to touch it, but she snatched her hand away and wrapped her arms around her knees, leaving my hand swinging through empty air.

"There's still a lot that I don't know about the world," I said. "If there are people who can calm down by cutting their arms."

"You're awfully haughty for a child."

"You know, I had no idea this place was here."

"I see."

"Do you always come here, Minami-san?"

My little friend had begun wandering the rooftop, her tail swaying, so I stood up to follow. As soon as I started walking, I realized how much wider the rooftop was than I had imagined. I came back, close enough to see the blood on Minami's wrist.

"What're you hanging around here for?" she asked. And then: "I only found this place recently."

"What are you doing here?"

I scooped my little friend up in my arms and spun around. Miss Bobtail cried out and I let her go. She wobbled as though the ground had gone out from under her, and flopped down at Minami-san's feet. I laughed.

"Don't pick on it."

"I'm not picking on her. We're playing."

Minami stroked Miss Bobtail's back, as though pleased by the black stripes of her fur. Hearing the cute, pleased mewl she let out, it occurred to me again what a wicked girl she was to resort to such flattery.

"So, what are you doing here, Minami-san? If I was coming to a big open place like this, I think I'd dance. How about you?"

"I don't dance. I just sit and look at the sky."

"And then you cut your arms. Now that I'm looking, I can see that you've cut them plenty of times...you really are going to die."

Minami-san looked at her arms and sighed. I had no idea what that was supposed to mean. Should I continue this conversation?

Her expression said both that she wanted to talk and that she didn't. I was sure that I had never made such a complicated expression. When I wanted to talk, I did, and when I didn't, then I didn't.

I reminded myself to ask Skank-san about the face Minami-san was making. If you wanted to know about adults, you should ask another adult. Instead, there was one other thing that I wished to discuss, so I turned my sights towards that.

"Hey, Minami-san."

"What? Shut up already."

"I was wondering if you like to draw pictures."

"What's this all of a sudden?"

I had spied the notebook and pen hidden away in her shadow. Perhaps she understood what I was getting at, because she quickly shoved the notebook under her butt and pulled a face, as if to say "You were just seeing things, there's no notebook there." But I was sharp enough to see through such lies. I pointed at her behind.

"Why do people who draw always hide it? There's a kid like that in my class too. He draws such wonderful pictures, but he hates people knowing it. Why do you hate showing off?"

For a few moments Minami was silent, staring up at the sky. But, as my little black-furred friend sprung away to chase a small white butterfly, Minami sighed again.

"It wasn't a picture." There was a pause, as though she was mustering her courage, before she spoke again. "I was writing."

"Writing? Were you writing in your diary?"

"No...I was...writing a story."

"Whoa! That's amazing!"

Minami averted her eyes, as though worried she would be smashed to pieces. But as the words leapt out of the bottom of my heart, she looked surprised. Maybe I'd let my voice get a little too loud again. However, I quickly saw that it was not my battle cry that shocked her. Something very peculiar had caught her surprise.

"You aren't...gonna laugh?"

I was unsure of what she meant.

"Laugh? Me? At what? Why would I laugh, when I haven't even read any funny jokes? If you're saying that I would laugh at people who write stories, then my stomach would probably twist up and kill me while I was busy reading. Why would seeing someone write a story be funny enough to make me laugh?"

She shook her head. For the first time, I glimpsed her eyes through her swaying bangs. They were beautiful, just like Skank-san's. And Granny's.

"That's not it!" she said, as loudly as I had.

I was not surprised. If I got surprised at things like that, I would shock myself so badly that I really would die. I decided to implore her.

"Say, let me read that."

"Huh?" she said, surprised again.

Obviously, if there was a story then I wanted to read it. But I knew that was not normal for a child of my age, so I could understand her shock.

"I've already said so, but I am clever. I know how wonderful stories can be."

"What's that supposed to...no!"

"Why not? Oh, do you have some other engagement?"

"I mean, I don't."

"Then please, let me read it. I know how wonderful stories are, and honestly, I've always thought that I'd like to write one of my own someday."

Minami's face showed not the slightest hint of movement, but the secret I had revealed seemed to grant her power. She pressed her hand to her mouth and grumbled, utterly resigned.

"Why do I gotta show this to some stupid brat I just met?"

She handed me the notebook.

I'm sure that Minami-san knew that a girl's secrets did not come cheap. I had not told anyone that I wanted to write a story before. Although I had grand plans of one day moving everyone with something I had written, this was the first I'd ever told anyone. In exchange, I secured the chance to read a brand-new story. I think that's what people call negotiating.

"Ah, wait."

"What is it?"

"I completely forgot. I'm reading about Homeless Huck right now."

"Huh, I read that when I was a kid, too."

"I've never read another story when I'm already in the middle of one. That's my rule. I want to be able to completely immerse myself in a world."

"Then give it back." Minami pursed her lips and took the notebook back. "I get what you mean, though," she muttered, placing the notebook back under her backside.

It was like a treasure chest she was hiding so no one could find it. It made me want to read her story all the more.

"I'll finish reading *Huck* soon! Let me read your story when I'm done!"

"I'd prefer you just forget about it."

"No, I won't forget. Life is like the contents of a refrigerator!"

"What the heck does that mean?"

"Even if you forget about the nasty peppers that are in there, you'll never forget about the delicious cake!"

Minami-san laughed, as though simply expelling air from her lips. "You're really something, brat."

I didn't get any bad feeling, like I was being badmouthed. Although she kept calling me "brat," which I knew was something that people said when they were being cruel, I got the same wonderful smell from her "brat" as I did from Skank-san's "little miss," and Granny's "Nacchan."

I suppose that Minami-san recognized me as a friend. It was probably because she enjoyed stories just as much as I did.

If only everyone in the world loved books, I thought, *then it might be a more peaceful place.*

No one could ever think about hurting other people if they knew about something as exciting as stories. And yet, given that she knew this, I still could not understand why Minami-san would cut her own arm. She still would not say much about it, but I could get her to speak about other things, such as books.

She knew about way more stories than I did. However, even she did not properly understand *The Little Prince,* and I realized how truly impressive Granny was, that she could solve questions that even a high school student could not grasp. Minami-san said that she liked the part about the fox in the desert.

"Well, I'll come back here again."

"You don't need to. But I mean, you can do whatever you want. I don't own this place or anything."

"I can't wait to read your story!"

"Whatever."

"Don't cut your arm anymore."

Minami-san said nothing, but waved her right hand to shoo me and my tailless friend away. As we carefully descended the stairs, Minami-san was still up there, watching the reddening skies.

Today, I had gained another destination for my daily walks.

"Happiness won't cooome, wandering my way sooo, thaaat's why I set ooout to find it todaaay!"

"Meow meow!"

By the time we made it down the mountain, there were no more children left in the little park. Instead, there was a lone adult, sitting on an unswaying swing with a terribly sad look upon his face. I was suddenly quite concerned for him. I felt like I had seen him somewhere before, but I could not recall who it was. But, as I went to approach him, I noticed my tailless friend moving on. I just ended up just heading home for the day.

When I arrived at home, I was surprised to see that, for once, my mother was home before me. She looked between the flier I had left on the table and her pocket planner, and gave me wonderful news about the observation day. I found a new resolve—I had to think even more seriously about happiness. I dove into my soft bed that night with my mother's promise locked safe inside my heart.

The next day, I was faced with a very difficult choice.

"Life is like a bowl of shaved ice. There're so many good flavors to eat, but you can't eat all of them. You'd get a tummy ache."

I had to decide between Skank-san, Granny, and Minami-san. If I went to see all of them, I would run past the curfew my mother had set. I could only visit two places at most. It was as difficult as choosing between strawberry, lemon, and soda-flavored ice.

"So why'd you come here?" Minami-san asked, drinking a bottle of barley tea with a sullen look on her face.

"Oh? Well yesterday you said I should do whatever I liked," I replied.

"Go play with your school friends."

"I don't have any school friends."

"Seriously? You really are a loner, huh?"

"That's not true. I do have friends. I have this little one, and you."

"You can't just decide I'm your friend."

She looked at the sky and let out a snort. I mimicked this, watching a bird flying above. I thought about how difficult it would be to sleep in a bed if I had wings.

"I came here because I don't know anything about you," I said. "I want to learn more."

"You don't need to know anything about me."

"That's not true either. Life is like a Japanese-style breakfast."

"What the heck does that mean?"

"There's nothing that you don't need to know about."

"What are you talking about?" she said. "You're really something."

"I'm not *something*," I said. "And I don't want to be 'something,' I want to be more clever."

"Weird for somebody so impressive to say they don't want to be."

"People who are impressive can't make time to go out with their families on Mondays, can they? There's no point in being that impressive."

That was all I said, but...

"You talkin' about your parents?"

I was surprised to hear her say this. She really *did* have a high schooler's smarts. However, I was loath to nod in agreement, so I was silent. Minami-san huddled up again, wrapping her arms around her legs.

"Might not be such a good thing to be so clever after all."

"That's not true. I want to be super clever! There's no way you can write a story without being sharp, right? I never knew that there was a tree called the 'baobab' before I read *The Little Prince*. I didn't know there were talking roses, either."

"There are no roses like that."

"What? Are you saying baobabs aren't real either?"

I began to grow uneasy. Not once in my whole life had I even seen a baobab tree. But then, Minami-san was a high schooler.

"Baobabs do exist. They're big trees that take over a hundred years to grow. People say that they're the biggest on Earth, and that they were some of the very first trees. I've also heard that God was angered by the baobab tree's jealousy once and turned the tree upside down, which is why its branches look like roots."

"Who was the baobab jealous of?"

"Of the palm tree, who was more slender; and the fig, with its fruits."

I was deeply moved by this.

"That's a unique and wonderful story. How like you, Minami-san."

"There're just myths. It's not like I made up those stories."

"Still, you're much more clever than I am, if you know all these interesting stories. I hope I can grow even more clever so that I can know them too."

"Hmph," said Minami-san, as though she had no interest in either me or the baobab tree.

However, I could tell that she was not unhappy. When I begged her to tell me more interesting stories, she had plenty to say. The most interesting one was that the phrase "under the rose" meant "secret" in English. I did not speak English yet, but I was sure that when I was an adult and I could, I would need to find a reason to use it.

I completely lost myself in talking to Minami-san that day. By the time I realized, it was already time to head home. I had completely forgotten to visit Skank-san or Granny. All the next day, I wanted nothing more than to talk with Minami-san again, but no matter how boring it was, I still had to go to school.

The idiot kids were still idiots, and my neighbor Kiriyuu-kun was scribbling secretively in his notebook, so school was as boring as ever. Still, at least there was one good thing. During break, while I was alone at the library, Ogiwara-kun showed up. I decided to strike up a conversation right away. I was dying to tell someone about all the things that Minami-san had said, but had no one else to spill them to.

Just as Ogiwara started to leave, not even noticing me at the far end of the library, I chased after him, making a face as though I was leaving, too.

"Ogiwara-kun!"

"Oh, Koyanagi-san. I didn't know you were in here."

"Yeah! What did you borrow?" I asked, pointing at the book in his hand.

He showed me the cover with a smile. I knew exactly what that expression meant. I, too, knew the joy of holding a brand-new book.

"*The Memoirs of a White Elephant,* huh? I've read that one too."

"Yeah, I wanted to read it when I found out it came from France, just like *The Little Prince.*"

Of course, that was Ogiwara-kun for you. He chose books the same way he laid the groundwork for our conversations. Taking advantage of this newly laid foundation, I told him about the baobab and the rose as though I had known them the entire time. Ogiwara-kun showed proper surprise for each. Surely, he and I were the only ones in our class who would find such things interesting. Because we were both clever.

We talked on and on, but I still was not satisfied. However, our conversation ended abruptly when a boy from our class called Ogiwara's name from the other side of the hall. Ogiwara turned and left as though he had forgotten we'd even been speaking. Of course that would happen. Not only was Ogiwara-kun clever, but he had plenty of friends.

I would have to find another outlet after school for everything trying to burst out from inside of me. Sitting under the blue sky on a concrete rooftop, I told Minami-san all about what had happened today.

"He's got your heart racin', huh?"

"I mean, we were just standing there."

"Not what I meant."

The corners of her lips were turned down again today, but that did not mean she was angry. Bit by bit, I was coming to learn about her.

"Oh right," I said. "I'll be finished with *The Adventures of Huckleberry Finn* soon."

"Yeah? And what about it?"

"Then I can read the story you wrote. I'm really excited for it."

"No idea what you mean," she said grumpily.

She was sitting on her notebook as always. She had probably been writing before I arrived.

"I'll see you next time, then."

"Do what you want."

Minami-san's "Do what you want" carried the same meaning as Skank-san's "See you later, little miss." I waved at Minami-san's back. After that, I stopped by Granny's home, and told her about the same things I had told Minami-san. It was a wonderful day.

Lately, I was attending language arts class with some rather complicated feelings. Although I looked forward to it, it felt sort of like standing at the bottom of a long set of stairs. It was the same feeling that the hero of a fantasy tale would have when facing down a massive dragon. I was the type to stand proudly before both steep hills and dragons, but there were children who would shrink back into their own shells. My neighbor was just once such child.

"Hey, what're you drawing there?" I asked Kiriyuu-kun.

"I, uh, nothing..." he replied, reluctant as always.

Although he was fine as a partner in group projects, I worried how he would fare as an ally on an adventure. Because he was my neighbor, we also ate lunch together. After that, I headed to the library alone and then, after school, I decided to head to Minami-san's building again. There was a particular reason for this.

"It's better to have lots of allies on your adventure."

"Meow."

Miss Bobtail seemed to enjoy Minami-san's company as well. Although we were completely opposite in appearance, our tastes in people usually aligned.

"You here again?" Minami said brusquely as we came out onto the rooftop.

Her words carried the same meaning as Granny's "Good to see you."

I sat down on the ground beside Minami-san, copying her huddled-up pose. "Salutations," I said. "I trust you are having a marvelous day?"

"What the heck is that about?" She returned my refined greeting by spitting her words out on the ground, but I had already figured her out. She worked very hard to sound that way. "It's not marvelous. Looks like it's gonna rain."

"It didn't sound like it was going to rain from the weather report. They said it was only a ten percent chance, which means that nine people said it wasn't going to rain, and only one person said it was."

When I started to think about one person standing against nine, I had the urge to cheer them on, but I couldn't do it. If it rained, I couldn't meet with Minami-san here.

"That's not what the percentage means."

"Huh? Really?"

"It's based on how many days it rained in the past on days like this one. A ten percent chance means that if you took ten days like this from the past, it would've only rained on one of them. It doesn't mean that one person was standing apart from their colleagues."

Once again, I was moved. That was Minami-san for you. I was thrilled to see that I had found the perfect ally for my adventure.

"I guess if I'm the hero then she's the fairy, and you're the sage living in the forest."

"What're you talkin' about?"

"There was something I wanted to ask you about," I said.

I launched into it straight away. I always was the type to eat the most delicious thing first.

"About my story?" she asked.

"I mean there is that, but this is something else. I'm dealing with a really difficult question in class right now."

"Is it a math thing? You need to deal with that stuff on your own, brat."

"That's not it. I can solve my own math problems. This problem is really hard. It is part of language arts class. The question was, 'What is happiness?'"

"Happiness..."

"Yeah. I wanted to ask what happiness means to you? It might give me some idea."

She did not answer me right away. She looked up at the clouded sky, stroking my little black-furred friend on the head. When she finally opened her mouth, her voice was clouded as well.

"I've never known happiness."

"Not even when you're writing? You aren't happy then?"

"Writing is fun, but I dunno if it makes me happy. I think happiness means being more fulfilled than that. Like your heart is full of good feelings."

She gave me an idea that was easily comprehensible. Only a

high-schooler could give such a reply so readily. I wished I could grow up more quickly.

"I see...so that's why I'm happy when I'm eating a cookie with vanilla ice cream on top."

This also meant that I was filling Skank-san's and Granny's hearts with good feelings just by showing up. I was so overjoyed, it felt like the sky might clear right then and there.

"Minami-san, when *does* your heart feel full?"

I looked at her arm. There was no blood today, but she quickly hid the scabs with her hand.

"Never."

"Does that mean you don't have any happiness?"

"Probably," she said, mimicking me, mimicking her.

"What about when you're reading books? Or eating sweets?"

"It's fun, and those are tasty, but I don't think that's happiness," she said, feigning gruffness.

"What about when you're eating dinner with your mom?"

"My mom and dad are gone."

"Gone? Do they live somewhere else?" *How typical of a high school student,* I thought.

"They're dead."

My tiny jaw dropped in shock. Minami-san forced my lips shut with her fingers and let out another sigh. She did not look me in the eye.

"They died. A long time ago, in an accident." Her fingers were gripping her skirt. "It's been a long time, so I don't cry about it anymore. Still, I think even a brat like you can understand why I'm not happy."

She still did not meet my eyes and so she had not noticed. But the little one sitting on her lap was looking right at me. I quickly placed a hand over her tiny eyes.

"So, sorry," she said. "But I can't help you with your home—"

Minami-san finally saw my eyes, and they silenced her. She saw my face and, in one clean movement, reached into her pocket and pulled out a handkerchief. It was not stained with blood today. She handed it to me.

I made use of it right away.

"You can keep that."

In the end, I was unable to say anything more that day. Looking at it later, the handkerchief she gave me had the same pattern as one my father bought for me once. I began to wonder if Minami-san's father had given it to her.

I left her behind and traveled to Granny's house, to find that she had baked sweets for me again today. However, before she offered me any, she asked "What's wrong, Nacchan?"

As I sipped the orange juice she'd poured, I told her about Minami-san. However, I avoided the parts that would bring up Minami-san's notebook and her precious story. I was worried that Granny might grow cross with me. I was a horrible child in that way. And yet, Granny offered me the financier cake she had made.

"I think that girl, Minami-san, is happy," she said mysteriously.

I shook my head with such force I'm surprised it didn't come off. "I don't think she is."

"No, she most certainly is. After all, she met you, the first person to ever cry for her. That's why she gave you her precious handkerchief."

I looked down at the damp, soiled handkerchief.

"So, there's no reason to worry so much over it. And there's no need to apologize to her. Still, I want you to promise me one thing, Nacchan."

I looked her straight in the eye and nodded.

"The next time you see Minami-san, greet her with a smile. If you like her, that is."

"I do like her!"

"Then you have to fill her heart up with memories of your smile, rather than all those painful things."

"I wonder if I can."

I felt unusually weak, but Granny placed her soft hands on my slim shoulders.

"People can't get rid of their sad memories. But if they can make lots of good memories, then they can live happily. Your smile has the wonderful power to do just that. For Minami-san, and for me."

"I wonder..."

I thought of Minami-san's face when she had handed me the handkerchief. I screwed my eyes shut, and thought with all my might—with my brain that was sharper than those of the other children, but not yet at the impressive level of an adult. And then, I made a decision.

I met the gaze of my little friend with her own shining eyes, then stood, displacing her from my lap.

"Granny, I'm going home now. I need to hurry up and finish reading *The Adventures of Huckleberry Finn!*"

"Aha, well if that's what you've decided, then you better go do it! What about your snack?"

"I'll take it with me!"

The sweet, tender financier tasted how I thought the sun would, if you made it into a dessert. And I realized that the sun had reemerged from the once-cloudy sky, as well.

On the way home, I saw that adult from before in the park at the bottom of the hill. However, I still could not remember who he was.

Chapter 4

A FEW DAYS LATER, after giving lip to the idiot boys, admonishing the cowardly Kiriyuu, and recommending the tale of Huck Finn to Ogiwara, I sat on the rooftop again.

I always visited around now, when Minami-san was there. I looked up to the sky and let out a deep full-bellied breath, as satisfied as if I had just eaten a big hamburger.

Minami-san stared ahead the whole time, stroking my fine-furred friend on the back. I thought as hard as I could about how to put the feelings that had come flooding from the bottom of my heart into words. Then I turned to Minami, who sat beside me.

"Life is like a goat."

"What the heck does that mean?"

"When I read a wonderful story, I could just eat it right up and it would nourish me."

"I don't think that's true."

"Huh? But I feel completely full right now, and I just read a wonderful tale."

Worried that my whole body would burst with the excitement, I took a deep breath and, as I breathed out, I called out to Minami-san.

"Minami-san! You're amazing! I can't believe you could write a story like this! You're incredible!!!"

I offered her my utmost respects.

As I had told her before, I had dreams of writing my own story someday. However, I had one other secret. In fact, I had already tried writing plenty of stories in the past. But whenever I tried, it never came out right. I could never bring characters like Tom or Homeless Huck into the world. It made me depressed, as depressed as if one of Granny's muffins had gotten stuck in my throat. At this rate, I wondered if I might just wither away.

To me, Minami-san, who could pen such shocking turns and such compelling characters, was more impressive than any important person on TV. I couldn't help but want to know how to write a story like this. Minami-san, however, suddenly went quiet, and would only say, "I see," no matter what I said to her.

"I wish everyone could read this story!"

"No way. No one is ever gonna see this."

"What a waste. You've gotta have more people read this. Life is like an afternoon break."

"Because you get to eat a tasty lunch?"

"Because there's only so much time, so you've gotta fill it with as many wonderful things as you can. I wish everyone could read your story during their forty minutes."

"Enough with the flattery," Minami said.

Although I was speaking truthfully, she took the notebook from my hands. She never let me hold onto it for very long. Honestly, I wished I could take the whole thing home with me and finish reading the story there. I could only read it when I was up on the rooftop, and it had taken me days. She probably thought I would get it dirty with juice or ice cream or something, but I would never do such a thing. I preferred being tidy.

"Well, that's fine," I said. "That means I'm your very first fan. I'm looking forward to your next story, too."

Minami waved her hand, still not looking my way. Then she looked up suddenly, as though something was falling from the sky. "Oh yeah...you find your answer about what happiness is yet?"

Minami-san's story still had its clutches on my heart, but Hitomi-sensei had taught us never to ignore someone speaking to you, so I gave her a proper reply.

"No. I've thought of a lot of different things, but I still don't have an answer that'll surprise everyone, or impress Hitomi-sensei. Honestly, I don't have a lot of time. Apparently only having half our thoughts together is enough, so we have to present at our next class observation day, too."

"Yeah?"

Minami sounded as though she was truly paying attention. I felt the sounds seeping into me—it was a wonderful feeling. My little friend, lying on Minami's lap and having her belly stroked, looked truly pleased as well.

"If you think of anything," I said. "Let me know."

"It's not something you can come up with that easily. Although, well...lately I think I have been a little happier than usual, getting to spend time with this gal like this."

Miss Bobtail licked Minami-san's hand and meowed, although it was unclear whether or not she knew she was being praised. Whose eye was she hoping to catch someday with those coquettish glances?

Although I glared at my little friend, I was glad that Minami-san was happy. Everyone I liked should be happy, and everyone I didn't like should just disappear.

I noticed then that the scabs on Minami-san's wrists were all gone.

I stood up, stretching my arms out high as if to reach up to the blue sky. Right now, I was too small to even reach up to high shelves, but if I kept going, I might stretch myself out tall enough to touch the basketball hoop in our yard.

Seeing me stand, Miss Bobtail looked my way and climbed down forlornly from Minami-san's lap. Minami-san, of course, did not look at me.

"I'll see you next time then," I said. "Hurry up and write your next story, I can't wait to read it!"

"Do what you like."

"That's right! I still don't know what answer to give about happiness, but reading your story made me happy."

Minami waved to me again silently, or so I thought. But a voice, softer than my own childish tone, came as if carried on the wind.

"Thanks."

I left Minami-san's rooftop with my chest warm and my heart full, and decided to head to Skank-san's place for the first time in a while. I hadn't been there in a few days, but even those few days were far longer than Skank-san and I should have ever spent apart. Skank-san felt the same way. She was drinking coffee when she greeted me in her cake-like cream-colored building down by the river.

"Been a while, little lady. How've you been?"

"I've been keeping myself calm, but I've had lots of energy, too."

"I see? This little one's been a Jiji to your Kiki, then, huh?"

"Unfortunately, I still can't do magic. So, I'd say we're more like Charlie and Snoopy. Even if I'm a girl and she's a cat, instead of a boy and a dog."

"I'm sure you'll be able to do it someday. All right then, come in. Just so happens I've got some cake today, and milk too."

"I'll have some!"

As I sat in her apartment eating cake, I explained to Skank-san why I had not been there in some time. Then I asked her about Minami-san.

"I don't think Minami-san is weird in the head," I said. "She can write really good stories, too! But I think it's weird that she cuts her own body if her head is normal. Do you know why she'd do something like that?"

I saw the space between her brows tighten. Unlike my own eyebrows, Skank-san's were sharp, so sharp that I could imagine them making a *ka-shing!* sort of sound.

"Mm, people are like that sometimes. It's something you have to ask the person themselves about. They might want to see blood, or they might just be curious, or it might calm them down."

"She said that it calms her down."

"Yep, so did that help you understand it?"

"Not at all. I tried scratching my arm, just to see, but all it did was hurt and leave a red mark."

"Right? So really, I think that it's something only the person doing it can understand. But it's all right not to understand, particularly for you. When you saw this girl, you wished that she would stop hurting herself, right?"

"Yeah, I hate knowing that my friends are feeling hurt."

"That's right. I think if you understood the reason someone might hurt themselves, and you started doing it too, then I would want you to stop. So, there's no need for you to understand it. It's just like I told you before: I think it's wonderful for you to only be able to enjoy the sweet parts of the pudding."

"But...but Skank-san! I really want to understand how she's feeling!"

"Mm, of course." She held up a finger, just like Hitomi-sensei would. "Little miss, do you know what number I'm thinking of right now?"

At this sudden, strange question, I stared into her eyes as though I might be able to see through her skull. But I still could not do magic, and I could not see into her head, no matter how hard I tried.

"E-eight?"

"Wrong. The correct answer was twenty-four. You see? No one can magically look into someone else's heart. That's why humans have the power of thought. You want to know things about your friends, but you don't understand the feeling of wanting to cut your own arm. In that case, you have to think about it, about what she might be thinking. Then, you'll come to know it, little by little."

"Yeah, that makes a lot of sense."

"You really are a clever girl."

Skank-san praised me, but it felt a bit wrong. She was the one who was really clever, giving me such a straightforward answer. I watched her casual motions. She really was exactly how I hoped I could be in the future—the beautiful and clever Skank-san, sipping coffee. If only I could write stories like Minami-san and bake sweets like Granny too, then I would be the perfect adult. I wouldn't even have to do magic.

Naturally, I could not beat the sharp and wonderful Skank-san in Othello today, either.

"Good luck with your observation day," she said as I departed.

"Of course! I'll show them all my smarts," I replied, leaving the building and walking home beneath the setting sun.

As I walked along the riverside embankment with Miss Bobtail, who was still in high spirits from her milk, I thought of the rapidly approaching happiness presentation and decided to consult the evening sun. There was a chance that what Skank-san had said about thought might be a big hint.

I reached the stairs down from the embankment. I was walking thoughtlessly, so it took me a while to notice the boy approaching me.

"Oh, Kiriyuu-kun! Salutations," I called out.

"K-Koyanagi-san!" he replied, hiding behind the adult he was walking with.

Miss Bobtail hid behind me as well. I smiled, thinking how funny it was to meet so many acquaintances here, and realized something else fortunate: I had the answer to a question that had been plaguing me for some time.

"Good afternoon," said the man who was walking with Kiriyuu.

It was the man who I had come across a few times recently in the park at the bottom of the hill. Indeed, although I'd had no luck remembering who he was before, I realized that he was Kiriyuu-kun's father. I had seen him once at a sports meet, but that single encounter was not enough to fully remember him. I suddenly felt wonderful, as though something that had been stopping up my throat was finally removed.

"Good afternoon!"

I returned his greeting cheerfully. Kiyiruu-kun still hid behind his father. I really wished that he would stop. He made it seem like I was picking on him.

Kiriyuu's father was not wearing his horribly depressed face today. I'm sure he had all sorts of moods, just as I did, but today he was in good spirits. It was wonderful to see. The two of us conversed about all sorts of trivial things.

"I'll see you at observation day, then."

With those words of parting, the Kiriyuus and I went our separate ways. Other than one small "S-see you later," Kiriyuu-kun himself said nothing.

"Despite how he is, that boy draws wonderful pictures," I told my little friend later.

Miss Bobtail merely tilted her head, mewling dubiously. She probably had no interest in human boys.

When I returned home and said farewell to my friend, I was greeted by a strange sight. Not only had my mother gotten home before me, but she had already finished making dinner. On top of this, it was all food that I loved. I began to wonder if I had somehow gotten the date of my own birthday wrong.

I loved my mother's cooking. She was a busy person, so we usually had to buy our ingredients at the neighborhood super-market, but the food she made was exceptional.

I happily ate up my favorite dishes, but partway through I realized something strange. My mother was just watching me eat, not touching her own food. I wondered if she was merely embar-rassed at how I was stuffing my face, but that was not the case.

I looked at her. She looked back at me with a very serious expression and said my name. I got a very bad feeling from this. Adults only ever made serious faces when they had something unpleasant to say. It was different from Hitomi-sensei's serious expression. I had seen such a look on the face of a scarier teacher, demanding to know who had broken a window, and on my father's face when he forgot my birthday. Sometimes they made faces like that in the hopes of surprising you with some happy news instead, but such times were incredibly rare.

How wonderful it would be if my mother was putting on an act to surprise me! However, I knew that that was not the case when she began by saying "I'm sorry."

She told me that both she and my father would have to travel somewhere far away for business soon, and so even though they really wanted to go, even though they'd been looking forward to it, and were incredibly disappointed, they would not be able to attend class observation day.

For a second when she finished speaking, it felt as though the whole room went dark. In that darkness, I felt the pit of my stomach drop. Although my lips were pressed into a pout, I probably still could have eaten my Hamburg steak. But I did not. With that momentary darkened mood, all the feelings of excitement I had been storing up within me exploded like a coiled spring.

"But you said you would come!"

She already knew how loud I was, and so this did not surprise her. What did surprise her was that I was angry, something that had not happened in a long time.

Although I say "a long time," in truth I had been feeling this way for a while.

"Always! You're always breaking your promises! Father too!"

"I'm really sorry, but we have to go."

"Why do you always choose work? Why?!"

My mother explained the reason that her work was so important, very simply, so that even I could understand. However, that was not what I was asking. I realized that my mother didn't understand me at all, and there was nothing to be done about that. Still, she could have at least tried to think about it, like Skank-san had said.

And so, even though I should have known better, I said something that I absolutely should not have said.

"Then I wish I'd been born into a family with a mother and father who *didn't* have such important jobs!"

I could tell right away that I had hurt her. However, she was the same as me, and could not stop herself.

"There's nothing we can do about it!" she shouted.

I went straight to my room without taking another bite and crawled under the covers. Although I hadn't eaten all my dinner, I was not hungry.

I said that life was like a goat, but perhaps it was more like an alien, I thought. I knew for the first time that my stomach was not just full of stories and happiness, but also sadness and despair.

Still, it turned out that I was hungry after all, and late that night, after my parents had gone to bed, I snuck into the kitchen and ate some bread.

I could not eat a single bite of the breakfast my mother prepared for me the next morning.

I had that
same
Dream
again

Chapter 5

Not wishing to go home, I went back only to greet Miss Bobtail after school, heading straight to Skank-san's house with my backpack still in tow. We walked along our usual riverside path towards the square, cream-colored building, but did not sing as we usually did.

We climbed the stairs and headed to the end of the second floor, stood before the door, and pressed the doorbell. I heard the sound of the bell from within, but there were no other sounds. No matter how many times I pressed the button, Skank-san did not appear. Apparently she was out today. Nothing to be done about that. Adults were busy, after all.

We went partway back along the route home before heading toward the usual hill. This time, on the rising path through the park where we often saw Kiriyuu's father, I chose to turn right toward Granny's house. I had gone to see Minami-san yesterday, so I decided I should see Granny first today. I climbed the hill alongside my glossy-furred friend, dabbing the sweat from my forehead. If I could see a friendly face and chat with them, perhaps my heart would feel a bit lighter. However, Granny's home brought no joy to my heart either. No matter how many times I knocked on the great wooden door, I never heard any voice in reply.

I sighed and looked down at my tiny little friend. "All the adults have abandoned me," I said.

"Meow."

And so I had no option left but to visit Minami-san, the adult who was closest to me in age.

We descended the hill, and this time climbed the left-hand stairs. My little black-furred friend was as chipper as ever, springing along lightly. However, as the minutes ticked by, my own body felt heavier and heavier, as though I was being filled with lead balls.

When we opened the iron gate and climbed the rest of the stairs, reaching the clearing at the top. There sat the large, frigid box as always, as though it had simply been plopped down in the middle of the field.

When I entered the box and climbed the stairs, Minami-san was waiting for me. I sat down beside her, saying nothing. Miss Bobtail took up her usual position on Minami-san's lap. That was when I realized that Minami-san seemed different from usual. Although it was a bit rude of me, I pushed her bangs out of her face. Behind them, her eyes were gently shut.

"Minami-san?" I said.

She opened them slowly, as gently as opening a cake box. She met my gaze with only one eye.

"Yo."

"Salutations," I replied. "This seems like a really nice place for a nap."

"I had that same dream again..."

"Which dream is that?"

"A dream about when I was a child. I have it a lot. Was school fun today?"

"Nope, not at all."

"Figured. You don't look like you had any fun."

Although I did not think she was looking at me, she must have been watching secretly from behind her long bangs. I didn't wish to discuss how I was feeling, so I decided to change the subject. I figured that if we talked about something I liked, my face would light up enough that she would not be able to tell. Just as the scars on Minami-san's wrists appeared to be fading, I was sure those lead balls would disappear.

"I've been thinking," I said.

"About why elementary school isn't fun? You can't have fun all day long."

"That is true, but that's not it. I was thinking...what if you showed your story to one of those places that publish books?"

In a rare move, she looked directly at me with a startled look. "What're you sayin' all of a sudden?"

"I realized that the reason lots of people can't read your story is because it's only written down in your special notebook, which means that no one can read it without coming here. So, you should get it made into a book. Then your story will be in the library and I can show it to Skank-san and Granny."

"Who's this 'Skank'?"

"My friend."

"You've got some weird friends."

"She's not weird. She's a wonderful person. She works as a lady in a midnight court. Isn't that wonderful?"

Minami-san's mouth twisted up strangely. "Do you always hang out with weirdos?" she asked.

"Probably," I replied, mimicking her, mimicking me, mimicking her.

"You have a wonderful job too, Minami-san. If the people at the companies who make books read your story, I'm sure they'd be all over you. Then you could write stories every day. You could create another world in the hearts of people all around the world, just like Mark Twain, or Saint-Exupéry."

"Easy for a brat like you to say."

"And you can write books at home too, so you can have a family, and have a kid, and you could play with them, and go on trips with them, and go to their class observation days, and they would never be lonely."

Suddenly, every fragment of my heart came spilling out. She brushed it all aside with a gentle sigh. "Ain't that easy, brat."

"Yes, it's very hard. Writing wonderful stories, that is. That's why I want more people to know about you and the wonderful things you write."

She heaved an even deeper sigh than before. "Listen," she said, in a tone that could be read as either anger or sadness. "The stories I write aren't that amazing. I just like putting words on the page. There are people in this world who are way more talented than me. You'll realize that soon. The stuff I write just isn't that interesting."

She spoke as though she had just swallowed something bitter.

"I...could never be an author," she said.

I took in the meaning of her words in the most childish way. I tilted my head. "What you're saying doesn't make any sense."

"What about it?"

"You're already an author, aren't you?"

This time it was Minami's turn to tilt her head, but I could not figure out why.

"Authors are called that because they author a new world in people's hearts, aren't they? Which means that, while I'm not an author yet, you already are. You've created a wonderful new world in my heart."

Of course, even a child like me was aware that people worked jobs to earn money, and that people who were called authors received money from selling books. However, in truth, it did not occur to me that "author" was the name of a profession. The idea that writing stories and selling books were connected was beyond my imagination.

In my mind, authors were not people who sold books, but wonderful people who created worlds of the heart. As far as I was concerned, Minami-san's name was now firmly among them. Thus, what she said baffled me.

Minami seemed to understand this as well. She breathed in and out in silence, then she smiled just with her mouth. "That so?"

"It is. That's why we need to get your story made into a book, so that everyone can read it."

She offered no reply. Instead, she simply looked ahead, smiling. I was filled with happiness at the thought that she might make use of my idea, and formed the same expression as her, looking up at the sky as it unfolded.

However, this feeling of joy did not last for long.

"What is happiness?" Minami asked, just when I thought the sky above might just swallow me up. "Do you have an answer yet? About what happiness is?"

My eyes fell to the concrete floor, suddenly forced to recall the thing I had been trying to forget. "It's fine, that's over."

"So you found an answer?"

"No. But, that's over now."

"What the heck does that mean? Dang, and here I had an answer for you."

I was stunned to hear this. Even though I had tried to say I didn't care about this anymore, I couldn't help but be interested.

"What? Tell me!"

"But you said it was over now."

"Yeah it is, but I still want to know your answer!"

She looked meaningfully through her bangs and into my eyes, then away and out into the sky. She spoke her heartfelt words as though simply placing them on the rooftop.

"Having someone recognize you. To say that it's okay for you to be here," she said.

I tilted my head. "Here? You mean on the roof? Did you get permission from the building owner?"

"Probably," she said, mimicking my mimicry of her mimicking me when I mimicked her.

I still did not understand the meaning of her answer. I would just have to search for my own answer. As I told her about the new book I had started reading, the sky grew red and the wind grew cooler, and before I knew it I heard the faraway sound of a bell chiming.

"Yo, time to go home, brat," she said, but I did not stand, nor call to my four-legged friend as I usually did.

"Don't you have to go home?" she asked.

"I don't want to go home."

"Look, don't worry your folks."

"I don't care."

Minami-san giggled. "They mad at you?"

"They aren't mad. We had a fight."

She looked at me, still smiling.

How rude, I thought fleetingly, *there was nothing funny about this.*

"Listen, brat. When you get home, your mom's gonna be making dinner for you, like always. A delicious dinner, like it always is. And when you're eating it, you're gonna say just one thing: 'Sorry about yesterday.'"

"I don't wanna."

"You're a stubborn one, eh?"

"But she was the one who was wrong here."

"It doesn't matter what the reason for the fight was."

The way she was talking irritated me. "But it's a really big deal! Mother and Father are always, *always* breaking promises to me, saying it's because of work."

"Work is a lot more important than you think."

"I know that. It's super important. More important than your own children."

"That ain't it."

"Then why is it they always decide that their work is more important than their promises to me? It was the same way this time. She said that they can't come to my observation day because they have to go on a business trip."

"Wh—"

Just as Minami-san was about to say something, a strong wind blew up. The sudden breeze forced me to shut my eyes. When the wind decided it was finished playing with my long hair, I slowly opened them again to look at her.

It was only a few seconds. The wind had stolen but a few seconds. I had no idea what might have happened in that scant amount of time.

"Minami...san?"

She looked like a mimosa plant. I was sure she would shrink away if I touched her. The smile that she had been wearing had completely disappeared from her face. I was stunned at this unheralded transformation.

"What's...wrong?" I asked her clearly.

But she did not reply. She only shook her head back and forth, quietly. Perhaps she wished to say "It's nothing," but even a child could tell that it was.

"Hey, Minami-san?"

"Yo, Nanoka."

Her voice was trembling and she said my name in that trembling voice. It was the first time she had ever called me anything but "brat." I got a weird feeling. I did not know why she was shaking, nor why she had said my name.

"What's the matter?"

"Nanoka...promise me one thing."

She ignored my question. Instead, she faced me head on, gripping me by the shoulders. Seeing her straight-on, her eyes were a color I had never seen before.

"P-promise?" I repeated.

"A promise. Or, a request from me, anyway. Listen."

"What's going on, Minami-san?"

"Just listen. Just one thing. When you go home, you have to make up with your parents."

I couldn't understand the meaning of this request. I shook my head.

"Look," she continued. "I understand how you feel. I'm sure you're hurt, lonely. Knowing you, I'm sure you said something terrible. I know that you wanna stand your ground, that you can't back down. You still gotta apologize today. Tell them, 'I'm sorry.'"

"I-I don't want to. That's not—"

"You'll regret it forever if you don't!"

Her voice cut through me like the wind, and now I was trembling. I shivered, looked at Minami-san's face, and shivered once more. She was angry. For some reason, I got the feeling that her anger wasn't directed solely at me.

I was completely lost. Ignoring my distress, she kept talking, saying more things that I did not understand.

"I...regret it. I've always regretted it. Why didn't I apologize back then? Now we can never even have a fight again. They can never get mad at me again. We can never...eat dinner together... again."

"Minami-san...what are you saying?"

"I can never apologize to them. So, I'm begging you."

A tear cut down Minami-san's cheek. As far as I was aware, adults never cried simply to startle children. Perhaps she realized that she was crying, because she tried to conceal it—dabbing her eyes furiously with her sleeve.

"Listen," she said. "Life is a story that you write yourself."

Although she mimicked my usual words, I did not immediately understand. I tilted my head, asking what others usually asked me. "What do you mean?"

"With revisions and corrections, you can rewrite a happy ending with your own hand. Listen, I'm not saying that you should never have fights. I'm just saying that I wish I had known, back then, that making up is just as much a part of a fight as the fighting. But because you're so clever, I'm sure you'll understand. Your mother was just as sad as you were when she found out that she couldn't attend your observation day. She was just as disappointed to learn that she couldn't spend time with you. That's why she worked so hard to make all your favorite foods, to be sure that she could eat dinner with you. And I'm sure you can understand why your father always makes sure to buy things that you really want for your birthday."

I thought about what she'd said. About my mother, who would come home just to eat dinner with me before she went back out, even though she was not yet finished with work. My father, who traveled far away just to buy the plush toy that I really wanted, since none of the shops nearby had it. Hearing a warm send-off at my back as I left this morning, even though I had been too angry still to say a word, or eat any of the breakfast that had been made for me.

I remembered.

"I don't want you to lose a chance to ever see them again without having made up, like I did," she said.

At those words, I finally understood. I knew why she was crying.

"So promise me. It's okay if you can't do it today. Tomorrow's fine. But you *have* to make up with them. You can't turn back time."

She pushed her bangs away and looked me straight in the eyes. It was the first time I saw her whole face. It was as clear as Skank-san's, and as kind as Granny's. It was beautiful.

I was not the sort of child to make light of a request from a friend. However, nor was I so thick-headed that I could banish all thoughts of last night that easily. And so I thought about it. I thought long, and I thought hard. I churned the gears of my tiny brain as hard as I could.

What was right? What was clever? What was kind?

And then, when I had thought it through, I looked Minami-san in the face, and nodded. "All right. I promise."

The last tear fell from the corner of her eye. "Thank you."

"But you have to promise me something too," I said.

Now it was Minami's turn to look curious. "You want me to put out a book?" she asked.

"Yes, that too. But it's something else. I want you to promise me. You understand what happiness is, don't you? But you also told me that you weren't happy. I can't stand for my friends not to be happy. So, please. Rewrite your story too."

Seeing her cry, I remembered the handkerchief she had given me, and how I had prayed for her happiness. That my friends would always have a smile on their faces.

Minami-san was dumbfounded at my request. However, she grinned and nodded. "I promise. Yeah, it's a promise."

We put our little fingers together and curled them in a pinky swear, my golden-eyed friend watching over us. I'm sure that Miss Bobtail had no idea what was going on. Honestly, I still had no idea why Minami-san was so concerned about my mother. However, I did know why I needed to make up with her.

"See you later," said Minami-san as my friend and I departed the rooftop.

Normally, she only waved at us, but today she watched us leave. I was so happy that I grinned back at her. Today, Minami and I had become better friends than ever. I was thrilled.

I rushed home more quickly than usual. I could tell by the blue car parked outside the building that my mother was already home. I bid my little friend farewell, and took one deep breath. Then, I rode the elevator to the tenth floor where we lived, walked down the hall, and stood before our door. I took another breath. I had to open up my heart. Sadness, loneliness, hurt, and all those other bad guys—I had to push them to the edges. Then, I told myself, I could stuff myself full of good feelings. Again and again, I thought of Minami-san's face.

Once I was ready, I took several more breaths, then stopped with my lungs still full of air. Just like that, I unlocked the door, turned the knob, and let my voice ring out loud into the apartment, blowing all the air out from my chest.

"I'm home!"

It was afternoon break, after lunch. The classroom was normally filled with the boisterous voices of those idiot boys, but today, the adults' voices sounded like the tittering of little birds.

I already knew that it was class observation day, a special event, but when I actually arrived the atmosphere was far more unpleasant than I imagined. With no idea what to do with myself, I simply put my head down on my desk. Perhaps assuming that I was not feeling well, Kiriyuu-kun called out to me.

"K-Koyanagi-san...are you okay?"

"Yeah, I'm fine. Thanks for asking…"

"Is your mother coming? Or your father?"

Honestly, the one time he opens his mouth, I thought, but I held my tongue.

"Neither one could come. They had work."

"O-oh, I see."

"Did your father come today?"

"No, he had to work, so my mom came. It was his day off when we ran into you at the river that time."

Perhaps it was the joy of having his mother around that had Kiriyuu-kun so talkative? Frankly, I thought that was wonderful. I didn't wish to keep talking about painful things, so I decided not to ask him whether his father's job had anything to do with the park.

Finally, class began and Hitomi-sensei had us do our greetings. The chorus was louder than usual, and it was obvious that everyone else was showing off for their parents.

"You all have a lot of energy today," Hitomi-sensei said, so she must have thought it was out of the ordinary as well.

For today's lesson, we were to present our thoughts about happiness. One by one, starting from the front of the classroom, we stood and spoke about our thoughts.

Kiriyuu-kun and I sat in the last row, so we came last. Because we sat in the back, I could hear many of the parents chattering to one another, and I wondered why Hitomi-sensei did not admonish them for it.

I listened silently to the other presentations, wondering if one of them might give me some hint as to my own happiness.

However, they were of no help. All they had to offer were things like sweets and playing, all the ideas that I had already thought of and summarily discarded. I was not surprised to hear that Ogiwara-kun was the only to mention books.

As it grew closer to my turn, finally it came to Kiriyuu-kun.

I was an idiot to think he might mention drawing, to have even a sliver of hope about it. He stood timidly, his written composition in hand, and gave the same boring answer as the kid three places before him.

"Coward," I muttered.

I have no idea if my voice reached him as he sat back down. However, as usual, he said nothing. Now, it was my turn.

I stood slowly. I looked at the sheet Hitomi-sensei had handed out for us to write our answers. I looked squarely at the sheet, so that I would not misread it. The very first sentence of my composition was:

I still don't know what happiness is.

It was not that I had skipped out on my homework simply because my parents were not coming. I had thought long and hard about it. When I considered the answer Minami-san had given me, I just remembered her crying. Even so, I lacked the words to describe the shape of the feeling that had planted itself deep in my heart. I could not tell a lie, either. So I thought and I thought, and I settled on this.

I looked at Hitomi-sensei's smiling face, and at Kiriyuu-kun with his head hung, and Ogiwara-kun looking at me. I raised my composition in my hands and began to read. Or rather, I tried to.

Just then, there was the sound of someone running down the hallway. *Clack clack clack.* It was not the sound of the indoor slippers that any of us wore. Honestly, did adults forget that they weren't supposed to run in the hallways? I decided to ignore the aberrant sound and read my presentation.

However, I could not do that. The noise stopped just before our classroom, and the back door opened rudely.

Goodness, who is this interrupting my presentation? I thought, but instead of issuing a warning to this dreadful adult, a brilliant smile leapt to Hitomi-sensei's face.

"You're just in time!"

Just in time for what? I thought, tilting my head.

For some reason, Hitomi-sensei's beaming smile, which had been directed at the back of the class, turned on me.

On instinct, I turned to look. And then, I turned back around. Then, with the same expression on my face as on Hitomi-sensei's, I gave my presentation.

"My happiness is right here and now, with my mother and father here!"

Ah, I had broken my promise to Skank-san. And here I had told her that I was going to show my parents just how clever I was. I was unable to give anything but the answer I had come up with right on the spot, just like those other idiot children.

However, there was not a single lie. Because I had not prepared it beforehand, my presentation was shorter than everyone else's. Even so, Hitomi-sensei was beaming and applauding.

"I talked with your father about how much I wanted to go,

94

and we ended up getting the afternoon off," my mother told me that evening, as the three of us ate dinner together for the first time in a while. They had offered to take me to a restaurant, but I told them that I wanted to eat my mother's cooking. She forgave my selfishness with a smile.

I will have to thank Minami-san, I thought as I ate a big, tasty croquette, determined to head to the rooftop with my tiny friend as soon as school was over tomorrow.

The next day, I met up with my black-furred friend as soon as school ended, and headed for the hill. Normally at this point I would have to decide who to go see, puzzling over it like a menu at a restaurant, but today my destination was set.

As usual, there were smaller children running around the park at the bottom of the hill. Normally, I would be jealous of them spending time with their mothers at the park, but today was different. I already knew that my parents loved me.

I quickly chose the stairs to the left. The sun was burning with all its might, but was not the only cause of the sweat that dotted my forehead. It was because my head was burning with excitement at the thought of seeing Minami-san.

As I climbed the stairs, we passed by someone else. Could it be the owner of that building? If that was the case, I had to thank them for letting us use it all the time. However, I considered the possibility that he might get mad at us for that, and instead only said, "Hello," to the suited old man.

He gave me a strange look, but returned a gentle "Hello."

Why was it that adults always looked at you strangely when you greeted them, despite telling children that they should greet everyone they see?

Not long after that, the old iron gate came into sight. Normally it was open, but sometimes it was shut as though someone had come by to check on it.

Today, it was shut, and a sight I had not seen before unfolded before me. Normally, I could see up the stairs beyond, but today the stairs were hidden by two adults.

What was going on? I walked straight up to the adults to ask what was happening. One of the pair, a man who looked older than my father, turned to me.

"Sorry to interrupt your walk, little lady, but you can't go past here."

"Really? How come?"

"Up through here is a construction site. It's dangerous, so we can't let anyone through."

I tilted my head. "Construction?"

"There's an old building up at the top there. It's falling apart, dangerous, so it's gonna be torn down."

There was only one old building at the top of those stairs.

"Y-you can't!" I shouted, without thinking.

The adults looked shocked.

"Was that place a secret base of yours?" the man asked. "I'm sorry, but that place really is dangerous. If you play there, it might collapse right on top of you."

Secret base. That was the perfect word to describe the atmosphere of that place. I was so disappointed to only learn this most fitting term just as the place was about to be destroyed. More than anything, I feared the look of sadness on Minami-san's face.

"Say, did a high school girl come by here today?"

"A high-schooler? Nah, haven't seen any. Yo, you see anyone?" the older man asked.

The younger man just shook his head. "Were you supposed to meet her here?"

"Yeah, I was. So, was this construction decided by whoever owns the building?"

"Hm? Yeah, that's right."

Nothing to be done for it, then, I thought. Even a child knew that it was up to the owner whether something was to be treasured or destroyed. If possible, I'd hoped for it to be treasured, but no adult would care about the wishes of a little kid whom they had never even met.

I was incredibly disappointed, but I knew that I couldn't give up. "Hey, I've got something to ask you," I asked the kind, smiling old man.

"What's that?"

"If a high school student named Minami-san comes up here, can you tell her I'll be at the big house up at the top of the hill?"

"It's a promise."

I wrapped my pinky around the old man's and climbed back down the stairs with Miss Bobtail, heading for Granny's house.

I waited there all afternoon for Minami-san, eating Granny's sweets, but soon it was time to go home and she had still not shown up. She did not come the next day, or the next, and even though I told Granny to tell me if she ever showed up, it never happened.

A short time later, I traveled to the clearing where Minami-san's building had been, but there was nothing but rubble. The disappointment tasted like a bowl of corn soup without a single piece of corn in it.

I would never again be able to meet with Minami-san here.

That got me thinking about a number of odd things. The first was that, though we lived in the same town, not once had I ever passed Minami-san on the street, nor even a single high school girl wearing the same uniform. The second was that the handkerchief I had received from her, which I had stored carefully away in my desk, had vanished. No matter how hard I looked, I could not find it. I began to feel a despair that went beyond despair.

The final thing was the most peculiar. No matter how much I talked about Minami-san's story, I couldn't remember a single thing about it. I had been so moved. I had seen such a wonderful new world, and I remembered the feeling of deepest satisfaction, but no matter how deeply I searched my brain, I had not a single memory of the contents.

I knew from reading stories that mysteries were wondrous things, but the mysteries born from my time with Minami-san only left me scratching my head.

And that was how Minami-san and I came to part.

Chapter 6

SOON, A TYPICAL SUMMER was in full swing. The temperature rose, and I sat with Skank-san, eating ice cream and bathing in the wind of an electric fan.

"It's weird, when the breeze from the fan hits it, the ice cream always seems to melt faster."

"That's because when the wind blows, it sends all the warm air onto it."

"Even this cool breeze?"

"Cool as far as you're concerned. But it's still warmer than the ice cream, isn't it?"

I was so moved I thought my eyes might fall out of their sockets. Skank-san really was far sharper than I. However, not even she knew anything about why Minami-san had disappeared. It truly was a mystery.

"Life is like a watermelon."

"And what does that mean?"

"You can chew up most of it," I said. "But there are some little bitty parts that you still can't eat."

"Aha ha, that's true. But even if you can't eat them, you can still bury them somewhere for them to sprout into something new."

"Whoa."

"Say, little lady, are you full yet?"

"Not at all. Hitomi-sensei said that your appetite goes away in summer, but that's just another mystery to me, cuz when it's hot out I use up all my energy, so I have to eat lots!"

"Then I have a favor to ask of you. Could you run to the supermarket and buy us a wedge of watermelon?"

"I can do that!"

I proudly accepted the money from Skank-san and put my yellow socks back on. She would stay behind, freshening up for work. I loved ice cream, of course, but watermelon was one of my other favorite things. It was a wonderful thing that Skank-san loved the same things that I did.

"Maybe she was a ghost," said Skank-san.

She rubbed lotion into her face as I downed some barley tea before heading out into the afternoon sun.

"What do you mean?" I asked.

"Minami-san."

I had not even considered that Minami-san might have been a ghost. I tried recalling her face.

"But she wasn't see-through or anything. She had legs and stuff. I think if anything she's probably more like a Totoro than a ghost."

"Ha ha, I see. In that case, you'll probably see her again, while you're still a child."

That might be true, I thought. I couldn't wait for the day when I'd get to see her again.

"I'm going now!"

I donned my shoes, shoved the money into my pocket, and headed to the nearby supermarket with my little friend, who had been rolling around in the shadows.

It was fortunate that I drank that tea before heading out, I thought. Outside, it was sweltering, heat radiating from the sun and from the ground and the walls of the buildings as well. Without that tea, I might've shriveled up into a tiny mummy before I made it to the market.

My dark-furred friend, not suited to the summer sun, sought out the shadows. *That makes sense,* I thought, as she wore neither shoes nor socks on her four little feet. Of course, I had to carry her through the spots where there were no shadows. As I carried her, she sang all the while. "Meow meow!"

I sang along with her. "Happiness won't cooome, wandering my way sooo..."

"Meow meow!"

As we reached the supermarket, there were tons of people going in and out of the automatic doors. I could not help imagining the shop itself eating watermelon and spitting out the seeds. I became a bit of a roadblock as I stood there in front of the doors, enjoying the cool breeze that came out from within, like an exhalation.

"Okay, you wait right here now."

"Meow."

The nice shadowy spot that I found for her had a prior occupant: a large yellow dog with a collar around his neck, many times bigger than her. Not showing the slightest hint of fear, she sat down beside him. Suddenly aware of her presence, he looked at her and she looked at him, and for some time they carried on like that. Oh my, was this the start of a new romance?

Although I worried whether a wicked girl like her could truly bring happiness to an upstanding fellow like him, I decided not to interfere. I left them behind, and quietly entered through the automatic doors.

I greeted the security guard as always. The guard, who stood watch near the doorway just like a watchman from a fairytale, respectfully returned my greeting. Initially, I had assumed security guards were policemen out on an errand, but the elderly guard reminded me of a sorcerer and had explained once that guards were allies of justice, guarding the gates of this marketplace.

As I stepped within, a myriad of smells floated to my tiny nose.

I loved coming to bigger supermarkets. No matter how many times I visited, I always found things I had never seen before, never eaten before, and all of my favorite things buried among them. It brought me the same joy that I felt when searching for a wonderful book.

I found the watermelons quickly. There were round, uncut ones; and ones cut into triangular wedges. I found a wedge that was just big enough for me and Skank-san, and placed it into my shopping basket. There were also some square-shaped melons there. Having never seen such a thing before, I was shocked. Seeing how much money it would take to buy one of them, I quickly understood that even when it came to melons, things that were different were more costly.

Although I had already found what I had come here for, I decided to look around some more. I had no intention of interfering with my friend's romantic pursuits, and I wished to stay inside this cool place just a little bit longer.

I saw fish and vegetables, and as I looked at the recipe cards beside the baking supplies, thinking how I wanted to be like Granny someday, a voice suddenly called to me.

"Koyanagi-san!"

I turned around at the familiar voice. I wonder whether my face was as bright as that day's sun. "Oh hey, Ogiwara-kun! Here to shop?"

"Yeah, my mom sent me out here. You?"

"I came to buy some watermelon. It's hot out."

"Yeah, it's pretty hot today. I want to go out to some cold planet, like the Little Prince."

A very Ogiwara-kun reply, I thought. As far as I was aware, he and I were the only ones in our class who had read that book. I had not spoken to him since the time I told him the story about the baobab tree. At school, he was always talking to someone else, so I was thrilled at the chance to converse with him again.

We talked for some time about *The Memoirs of a White Elephant,* which he had finished reading. Was it five minutes? Ten? I quickly forgot that I had come on an errand for Skank-san.

I only remembered my objective when I looked down at the watermelon in my hands. While the idea of leaving gnawed at me, I could not keep my beloved Skank-san waiting. It was time for me to go.

Ogiwara-kun and I were not friends. We only talked to each other from time to time. We had never eaten lunch, or even a snack together. Plus, I was not the only one who Ogiwara-kun spoke to. He was like that with everyone in the class, even Kiriyuu. Even so, I was able to converse with him as easily as I could with Skank-san, or Minami-san. He was the only one in our class who was as clever as me.

My wedge of watermelon was growing lukewarm and I switched it out with another. Then I finally took my place in line at the register. After a short while in line, I handed my watermelon to the lady at the register and paid.

"Running errands?" she said. "That's impressive, little lady."

I did not think that was impressive at all. "Thank you, but I don't think that's true."

I got a white shopping bag and stuffed the watermelon into it. Then back to Skank-san's place...or so I thought.

I froze as I heard a loud voice.

I couldn't believe it.

It was just like a scene out of one of the mystery novels I had read.

The sound was coming from the entrance of the supermarket, a cacophony of loud voices. Startled, I looked towards the commotion to see two guards holding someone down. Nearby I saw another guard, pressing at his own face as though to check for injury. The loud voices were coming from the three people on the floor.

"Don't move!" one of the guards yelled, as incoherent shouting echoed through the supermarket.

I had no idea why, but the person on the ground sounded like they wanted to hurt someone. I could not will my legs to move.

What was going on? I didn't understand, but I was quite uneasy. I churned the gears inside my little head.

"Must be a shoplifter," said one of the adults nearby.

A shoplifter? I knew what that was. It was a thief.

Had that man been caught stealing? That much I could understand. Even though I understood this, I still could not bring myself to move.

It was only when the guards warned off the people standing around snapping pictures on their cellphones that my legs decided to move. At the time, I still did not have a phone of my own. Even if I did, I had no interest in taking photos of bad people. I could not see their face, but there was no doubt that they were scary. The thief was taken away, but the murmuring around the store continued.

People scattered like a swarm of ants, and I took advantage of the opening to make my exit. I wished I could have left this place just a second sooner, before such a scary thing had happened. I glanced over as I left, seeing dots of red where the battle had occurred. I quickly averted my eyes and rushed outside, my chest heaving with breath. I desperately needed to open up that window into my heart. That warm air soaked lovingly into my chilled thoughts.

"Meow."

I looked down to find my little friend looking my way, almost glaring. The yellow dog was already gone.

"What's that look for? I didn't forget about you. A lot of things happened in there. Let's get back to Skank-san's place."

I tried my best to forget what had just happened and I walked with my disgruntled friend in tow. I sang, carried her even when it wasn't necessary, and asked her about the yellow dog. Still, a fog lingered over my heart. It felt very much like the time I heard my mother and father shouting at each other.

I had the courage and the righteousness to admonish people when they were doing wrong. If I'd seen that person stealing, I surely would have said something. So why was my heart so hazy to see them apprehended? I couldn't understand. I had witnessed something dreadful. That was all I could feel.

This haziness continued even after I arrived back at Skank-san's place. I ought to have asked her about it while she was chilling the watermelon for us. However, I had no interest in talking. I didn't wish to put it into words and find those sights and sounds floating back up to the surface of my mind. Thus, I decided to only talk about pleasant things.

"I saw a boy from my class at the market. We talked for a bit."

"Oh, you made a friend in class? I'm so glad to hear that. I was worried that you didn't have any friends at school."

"He's not a friend. We never talk about anything important, or meet up to hang out. Plus, I already have you, and this little one, and Minami-san, and Granny."

"You should make friends with the kids in your class, too. Just like me, and Minami-san, and Granny. Why don't you?"

"That's easy. There's too much distance between our hearts."

Skank-san opened her mouth as though to say something, but stopped herself. "I see," she said at last, with a thin laugh.

For some reason, as I continued to speak, the smile on her face grew wider and wider.

"That boy isn't my friend, but I like talking with him. He's smart and he knows a lot about books. I wish I could talk to him more, but he's nice to everyone. I wish he'd talk more to me, instead of to all those empty-headed idiots in our class."

"Oh?" She stopped lining her eyebrows with a pencil and looked at me. The look on her face was not the sparkling smile she usually wore, but a sly grin. When adults made faces like that, they were always thinking something devilish. "I think you really like that boy."

"Yeah, well, I guess even I can like a classmate sometimes."

There was one more classmate I might be able to like if he could just grow a spine, but there was no sign of such a thing happening. Class observation day aside, he only ever ran away from me.

"That's not what I mean," she said.

"It's not?"

"You're in love with that boy, aren't you?"

I'm sure I was just imagining it, but I could feel my whole face about to burst. "No way. I don't even know anything about him."

"That doesn't really matter."

"Love means you want to marry someone, doesn't it? I definitely haven't thought about that."

"Marriage isn't all there is to love."

"What is love, then?"

"I don't really know. I'm sure you'll understand it though, with that sharp brain of yours, little lady."

I could not conceive of the idea of there being something I knew that Skank-san did not. I knew that love and marriage existed. However, I had no interest in running away with Ogiwara-kun as the lovers in stories did, nor did I wish to gaze deeply into his eyes. I just wanted to talk to him.

As we ate the watermelon, I decided to ask Skank-san a question. "Is there anyone who you want to marry?"

"Nope. I don't think I'm really the marrying type."

"Why not?"

She looked up at the ceiling and hummed to herself, thinking, before she replied.

"It's like a crème brûlée. It's fine that you can only see the sweet parts of love when you're a child. In fact, it's absolutely wonderful. Everyone knows that. But when you're an adult, you realize that the bitter parts of the pudding are there as well, and sooner or later, you will have to eat them. But it's not like coffee and beer. I hate the bitter parts of love. But it's a lot of work to avoid them, so eventually I just stopped wanting to eat it at all."

"This is complicated."

Far more than math, or cooking, I thought.

"I mean, there's plenty of people who don't get married these days, anyway."

"I don't think I'll get married when I grow up, either. Life is like a bed."

"What do you mean by that?"

"A single is enough for sleeping."

Skank-san stared at me for a beat, and then gave the greatest laugh I had ever heard. I was thrilled that she enjoyed my joke, and munched the watermelon joyfully.

"Was that meaning intentional?" she asked me.

Not understanding the question itself, I just tilted my head.

That night, as always, I grew sleepy around ten o'clock, mulling over all sorts of things. I snuggled into my warm bed and went to sleep.

The next day, when I arrived at school, an unfathomable rumor was going around: Kiriyuu-kun's father had been arrested for stealing.

There was no way that such a kind man could have done such a thing, I thought. I wanted to force Kiriyuu-kun to say that this was a lie, but this turned out to be impossible.

Kiriyuu-kun had not come to school that day, and when I asked Hitomi-sensei about it, I was unable to learn a thing.

For the next few days I was without my usual partner. While Kiriyuu-kun was absent, I paired up with Hitomi-sensei during our ongoing happiness discussions. I did not dislike this new arrangement. In fact, I relished it, but I still could not help but be concerned about the rumors surrounding Kiriyuu-kun. I was particularly concerned because if the rumors were true, there was a chance it was related to the scene I had witnessed. And Kiriyuu-kun's gentle father did not appear to be the sort of person who would do such a bad thing.

It was six days, with the weekend in between, before Kiriyuu showed up at school again. When I migrated from the library to the classroom, just before Hitomi-sensei's arrival, I saw him climbing up the stairs.

"Good morning, Kiriyuu-kun."

I waited until he reached the same level as me before greeting him. Perhaps he did not know I was there because he looked at me, eyes wide and shoulders trembling. He looked like he might jump out of his skin on the spot.

"K-K-Koyanagi-san."

"Been a while. Were you on vacation?"

I could only hope. However, he just hung his head, and gave no reply.

"I understand how you feel," I said, and when he did not respond, I kept talking. "It's really hot in Japan right now. I wish I could go somewhere cooler."

He lifted his face a little and looked at me, but still said nothing.

When I entered the classroom, no one said anything to me as usual, or even looked my way. However, when Kiriyuu-kun came in, all conversation stopped and all eyes turned on him.

It should have been a blessing, having everyone's attention on him, but instead it felt like a cold wind. I wondered if Kiriyuu might just freeze to death. Despite my worries, there was no chance for this to happen as Hitomi-sensei soon entered. That was just like her, always punctual. As she came into the classroom, greeting us loudly and drawing the class's attention, Kiriyuu and I took the opportunity to slip to the back and take our seats.

I thought that Hitomi-sensei might have some explanation as to why Kiriyuu-kun had been out of school, but she did not say anything. She gave her morning announcements as though Kiriyuu had not missed a single day, then left the classroom again.

"Hitomi-sensei!"

I ran after her as she departed. She did not show the same surprise that Kiriyuu-kun had earlier. Perhaps she knew that I was following her, and that I wished to ask her a question. She smiled when she turned around, but I could see the sort of serious expression adults made when they had something unpleasant to say.

"What's the matter, Koyanagi-san? Are you having trouble looking over your math homework for next period?"

"No, my homework is perfect. But Sensei, there's something I want to know."

"What...?"

"It's about Kiriyuu-kun."

Although she was still smiling, she bit her lip and took me to an unoccupied classroom down the hall. I never minded having a secret conversation.

She crouched down to meet my eye, and whispered in a voice much softer than usual. I was finally going to learn something. I listened with rapt attention.

"Have there ever been times when you didn't want to come to school?" she asked.

"Every day," I replied. "But I still come, because I want to grow smarter. And because I like seeing you."

She gave a complicated smile. "Well then, I'm sure you have days when you absolutely don't want to come, like the last day of summer vacation, and Mondays, right?"

Surely enough, there were plenty of times at the end of weekends and vacations when I had wished that I could use magic, and so I nodded. When I did, she nodded back.

"Right? So it takes a lot of courage and power of heart to come to school on those days."

"And delicious sweets."

"Yes, indeed. So, even though Kiriyuu-kun had to take some time off from school to do some important things, it took a lot of courage and heart for him to come back today after all that time away, you know?"

"I get it."

All the more for a coward like Kiriyuu-kun, I thought.

When I nodded, she smiled happily.

"I might be able to prepare some delicious sweets for later, but in the meanwhile, Kiriyuu-kun will need allies in the classroom to help him summon up that courage and strength. I want you to be one of those allies."

"But I was never his enemy."

"That's true. So I want you to stay as you are, then. Just talk to him, and sit next to him, and eat lunch with him, like you always do. Can you do that?"

"I can do that much. It's not like he's sprouted a horn out of his head."

She tittered. Her expression was like the one she had worn when I gave my presentation on observation day. "I'm glad I can count on you. If Kiriyuu-kun still seems like he's having a hard time, even with your help, come and tell me, okay? He probably won't be able to tell me himself."

"Because he's spineless."

"That's not it. He couldn't have come to school today if he wasn't courageous."

Kiriyuu-kun? Courageous? I could not accept this from her words alone, but I still nodded and bid her farewell.

What was this important business that Kiriyuu had needed to attend to? I pondered it as I returned to the classroom. I decided to ask him about it later. Hitomi-sensei told me to act normal around him, so that much should be fine.

When I entered the classroom, I could feel a chilled air circulating around Kiriyuu-kun. I approached him to break through that cyclone.

"Excuse me," I said, pushing aside Kiriyuu-kun's drooping bangs.

He looked utterly shocked, but I had cleanly parted his hair, allowing me to get a clear look at his forehead. Sure enough, I found nothing there. I took my seat, and he looked at me with surprise and curiosity.

"Hitomi-sensei was making such a serious face I was worried you might've sprouted a horn. It's good that you don't have one. Sorry for the surprise."

Even as I gave a clear explanation for my behavior, the shock and curiosity did not drain from his eyes. He was the same cowardly Kiriyuu-kun as always.

I decided I would ask him about his important business when it was time to go home. I was always alone at the end of the day, and so was he. All I had to do was pull him aside and ask him. Or so I thought, but life is just like a father.

In other words, you never get your way.

"Yo, your dad's a thief, isn't he?"

It happened during afternoon break. Usually after lunch, when Hitomi-sensei was away and the classroom was noisy, most of the children went to play out in the yard, or to the music room to toy with the piano. But today, several chose to stay and pay a visit to Kiriyuu-kun. Naturally, it was those idiot boys.

Normally I would jump directly into the fray, but for now I chose to watch and let things run their course. Whether the rumors about Kiriyuu's father were true or not, I knew that people were going to be saying bad things about him from now on. *If only he had courage,* I thought, *he would be able to stave off these terrible things on his own.*

I held off on starting a fight to see what Kiriyuu-kun would say, but all he did was hang his head, like always.

This is no good, I thought. These boys' idiocy was such that, if their opponent said nothing, they mistook it as a sign that they were righteous.

"I heard from my mom that your dad was caught stealing from a supermarket in Ni-chome."

I pondered this as I watched Kiriyuu-kun's face. Sure enough, the scene I witnessed at the supermarket had become attributed to Kiriyuu-kun's father. Still, I did not know if it was true.

Kiriyuu said nothing and looked at no one, still hanging his head.

This did not please the idiots.

"Makes sense some picture-drawing weirdo would have a bad guy for a dad."

Still Kiriyuu-kun said nothing.

"Oh yeah, when Takahashi's ruler went missing, bet that was your fault, wasn't it?"

Nothing still.

"The son of a thief's gotta be a thief, too. Glad I wasn't born into a family like yours."

Ah, sorry I can't keep waiting, Kiriyuu-kun...

"Are you all really that stupid?" I said.

The idiots' eyes fell on me all at once.

"Oh? I don't believe I said *who* was stupid. I guess you all realized it yourselves."

"Huh?"

The boys—the chief idiot in particular—glared at me. I wasn't afraid. What I felt towards Kiriyuu-kun was far stronger

115

than that. I took it out on those boys instead, but the one I really wished to shout at was Kiriyuu-kun.

You coward.

"The child of a thief is a thief? What evidence do you have of that? Did you really think that 'thief' was the name of an animal or something? By that logic, that must mean that your mother and father are both idiots, the same as you. But they aren't idiots. I'm sure even an idiot like you had a proper upbringing—which means that you turned into an idiot all on your own. I feel sorry for your parents, to have such a huge idiot for a child."

The boy's face was growing redder and redder. He was angry. Even his reactions were idiotic. Still, I preferred his reaction to Kiriyuu's. He still could not find it in himself to grow angry, even when the people most precious to him were being ridiculed. It was only my promise to Hitomi-sensei that kept me from saying any of this to Kiriyuu-kun.

The idiot boys looked as if they were ready to throw something at me. But unlike them, I was clever. I had plenty of words to throw back.

"Anyway, it's just a rumor that Kiriyuu-kun's dad stole something. You all really are idiots if you'd believe any old rumor without any proof."

"But people saw him!"

"But you didn't see him, did you? So those people might've mistaken what they saw."

"This is none of your business!"

"Oh? But it isn't your business either, is it? Even if it *was* true—"

As all the words inside of me came spilling out...

"Stop it!"

A loud voice rang through the classroom. At first, I had no idea where it came from. It wasn't my voice. It wasn't the idiot boy's voice. It was a voice I had never heard before.

Just as I realized that the voice had come from Kiriyuu-kun, I also realized that he was, for some reason, looking up at *me* with those tragic eyes.

He was telling *me* to stop.

As I stood there, not comprehending why he would have said such a thing, Kiriyuu-kun stood up violently—his chair clattering to the ground with an echoing sound.

Then, while the sound was still ringing, he left the classroom without saying a word. After that, everyone fell silent. Even the blackboard and the desks and the chairs were holding their tongues. That was how quiet the room was.

Even as fifth period began, Kiriyuu-kun did not return. Even as afternoon announcements drew to a close, there was no sign of him.

Hitomi-sensei pulled me aside, and I told her plainly about what had happened during break. I also told her that, despite my fighting in his place, it was me he was glaring at when he left. When I asked her about what I should do, she told me that she would try talking to Kiriyuu-kun, and then sent me home.

Kiriyuu-kun was not at school the next day.

Nor the next day, or the next.

One day, Hitomi-sensei pulled me aside again and told me that Kiriyuu-kun would not be coming back for some time.

"Don't worry, Koyanagi-san," she assured me, "It wasn't your fault."

Still, I knew. Whenever an adult talked to you in that way, they really meant: "You weren't entirely wrong, but you were still responsible."

Even though all I had done was step up on his behalf. As usual, she was slightly off the mark.

It was raining. I went to Skank-san's place and told her about everything that had happened. I apologized for not saying anything on the day I went to buy the watermelon. I told her, honestly, that I hadn't wished to put it into words.

She was not angry at me for keeping quiet. When she heard my tale, she gave a nod that told me she understood.

"You must've realized it," she said.

"Realized what?"

"That adults are frightening."

Probably so, I thought. *That was probably why I had felt the same way when my mother and father were fighting.*

I also told her there was a chance the person who was caught might have been the father of one of my classmates. Although I'd said "might have," judging by the way Kiriyuu-kun was acting in the classroom, that question had been answered.

I told her about what kind of person Kiriyuu's father was, about his kindness and seeing him in the park. She let out a sigh.

"I see," she muttered.

"Why would he be stealing? And from a supermarket?" My

father would have been able to buy whatever he liked from a supermarket. After all, the most expensive thing were those square watermelons.

"Do you know something about that, Skank-san? Why he would've done that?"

Lately, my little head had been fully occupied with that question. Why, *why*? That word swirled around in my skull. Why would he have done that? Why had Kiriyuu-kun looked at me that way? I thought that if Skank-san understood, then she could explain it to me.

However, she shook her head. "Hmm, I wonder."

If she did not understand, then no matter how hard I thought about it, I probably wouldn't understand either. I was a little disappointed.

"But..." she continued. "Well, this is just a theory, but..."

"Huh?"

"It's just my own theory; it's not the truth. But would you like to hear it?"

"Please tell me."

"That man—the man who was stealing—he probably wanted out."

"Out? Of what?"

"Of his everyday life. Nothing matters to him anymore, so he wanted out of those never-ending days."

"I don't get it."

"You don't need to. It's fine for you not to know, little miss."

"Do you get it, Skank-san?"

Skank-san did not reply. Instead, she asked me if I would like to eat some gelato. I happily accepted the orange gelato, but there was something strange about it. The flavor seemed much weaker than before.

We talked about my classmate and my one remaining concern about the thief. I talked about the fact that Kiriyuu got mad at me, even though I had fought on his behalf, because he was so spineless. I told her that I did not understand why this happened, and that I did not know what to do for Kiriyuu, who was not even coming to school. Even though I had been his ally, just as Hitomi-sensei asked.

Although this was a serious concern for me, for some reason Skank-san laughed. I tilted my head, wondering if she had mistaken something for a joke.

"Sorry, sorry," she said. "You know, when I was a child, I was just like you. If I was unhappy about something, I started fights for people before they could do so themselves. If I had to put a finger on it, it was the kids who couldn't talk back who annoyed me the most."

"That's exactly it!"

I was thrilled to hear that I was like Skank-san when she was little. I wished I could hear more about her childhood. What kind of family did she have? What kinds of friends? Did she have any strange habits of speech, like I did?

"I was the type to always speak my mind, just like you. I don't really know what Kiriyuu was thinking. I can imagine, but I don't know whether it's true."

"I'd still like to hear it, if you don't mind."

"Hmm?" she said, tilting her head. "No, I won't say."

"Why not?"

"You want to try and make up with him, don't you?"

"I guess. I mean we never really got along that much in the first place."

She tittered again. "You really are like me," she said quietly. "If you don't care too much about making up with him, then you don't have to think too much about his feelings."

That was true, I supposed. I had no idea why I was even putting that much thought into it, so that sounded like a fair answer.

"Given how much you've already been thinking about this, you should come up with your own answer and then decide what to do. That's why I'm not going to tell you what I'm thinking."

She gave me a devilish look and crossed her lips with her finger, although she muttered softly behind it.

"Because I gave up," she said, so quietly I was unsure if I even heard it.

"Okay. I'll think about it myself. But you know, life is a like a ghost."

"And what does that mean?"

"There's always a hint."

As I drew the letters with my finger in the air, she immediately deciphered what I was trying to say.

"A haunt? As clever as ever, I see," she praised me. "So, a hint? Well I can give you a hint. Not for the answer, but for how to think about it."

"Okay."

"Ready?"

She held up her index finger and drew close to me. I felt my heart skip a beat, seeing those elegant, rouged lips drawing so near. I listened closely.

"Everyone is different. But we're all the same."

"Huh?"

I made a strange face. I must have looked very silly, with my lips pursed and my brows knitted together, because she laughed. I'm sure that if I had seen myself in a mirror, I would have laughed too.

"That's weird," I said. "That's like...what is it, something about the strongest spear against the strongest shield."

"A contradiction."

"Right, that. Different, but the same..."

The inside of my little head was spinning so quickly I thought my eyes might spin.

"Yes, it is strange. That's why my hint will guide your thinking. I'll go one step further and give you this: You're a child and I'm an adult, but we both like Othello."

"Hmm, I'm gonna have to think about this a lot more."

"Yes, keep thinking about it, and come up with an answer all your own. It would take too long for me to come up with that, but you're kind and clever, so I'm sure you'll do fine."

"Could I really get something that even you don't really understand?"

"You'll be fine. You know what? I'm sure that Granny could give you an even better hint. You should go ask her about it."

"I'll go tomorrow, then. I don't go to her house on rainy days. I get all muddy."

Skank-san smiled gently, looking up at the sky outside the window. "I hope it's clear tomorrow."

I truly did as well.

The next day, as if her prayers had reached it, the sky granted the sun's light to the Earth, clear and unabashed. Even the soggy ground had firmed up by the time school let out, and neither my favorite shoes nor Miss Bobtail's fine coat ended up dirty.

We took the right fork on the path leading up the hill. Although I was glad for the clear weather, it was growing hotter and hotter every day, and I began to worry that I might just dry up from sweating so much. I tried to magically shorten the path to Granny's house, but then I remembered that I could not do magic.

The shadows fell thick over the mountain path, and my little friend bounded up the hill with far more gusto than she had when walking the concrete city streets.

Finally, I thought as we arrived at the house and I rushed to knock on the door. It was only then that I noticed there was a slip of paper pinned to it. I read the words out loud for the benefit of my energetic little friend.

"Nacchan: the door is unlocked. Come in whenever you like."

I looked down into my friend's golden eyes, then wrapped my hand around the doorknob. Just as the note had said, the door opened easily.

"Hello!" I greeted as I stepped inside, only to find the house quiet.

Normally I would hear Granny and smell the sweetness of her baking, but today I sensed neither of those.

"Wonder if she's out?"

"Meow."

I wiped Miss Bobtail's paws with the damp cloth that had been placed at the front door and we entered together, but we could hear nothing besides our own footsteps.

First I headed to the living room, where the sun always shone brightly. I would often find Granny there, drinking tea or reading a book. However, the room was empty. Without her presence, the space seemed far larger than usual. I usually enjoyed open spaces, but there was something peculiar about this. All the room did was incite a sort of murmuring in my heart.

I did not enjoy that feeling, so I decided to head to the kitchen. Maybe she was cooking something that did not produce any sounds or smells. However, there was none of that, either. There was no one present in the orderly kitchen, and the emptiness and quiet of that place only riled my heart further.

It seemed that she was not home. Perhaps she had gone out shopping. I once again looked my tiny friend in the eye, and we continued down the hallway to the living room, as though that had been the plan the entire time.

It was difficult for the sun to reach that dark hallway, and for just a second I wished to get out. However, I had read plenty of stories, and I knew that if you ran at a time like this, whatever scary thing was after you would just catch up faster. So I proceeded down the hallway step-by-step, silently shouting that there was no fun in chasing me.

We passed by a number of rooms, but most of them were empty. They had cabinets and shelves, but beyond that they were deserted, no traces of human life. It seemed like Granny's family might have lived here once. Whatever had been inside those rooms had left along with her family. Now there were only empty shells. The only room that was not empty was Granny's bedroom. I had been in that room plenty of times. There was Granny's bed and her bookshelf, which she had taken books from to show me.

Just as I passed her bedroom door, my feet suddenly stopped. *Perhaps she is sleeping in bed,* I thought. I called out to my little friend, her fur blending in with the dark of the hallway, and knocked on the paneled glass door. I opened it, but as it turned out, she was not there either.

We should have left the room immediately and headed back to the warm, sun-soaked living room. Instead, I just stood there, stock still.

There was a particular reason for this. Eventually, I entered the room, opening the curtains. As a little light seeped in, I could distinguish the objects in there. The colors of the item I had spied seemed to take on a life of their own.

It was fixed to the wall. I took one step closer, and then another. In those few seconds I forgot all about my little friend, and perhaps even Granny as well.

"It's so pretty."

I was too young to know how to write the complex characters of the word *kirei*—"pretty." Instead, the word was imbued with all of the images scrawled invisibly on my heart. I had only intended to utter it silently, but my feelings seemed to have slipped out.

It was a painting, a beautiful one, layered heavily with color. It overflowed with such power. I felt it might suck me in entirely. I could not draw my eyes away. Perhaps I had in fact entered the world of that painting, if only briefly. I only realized that Granny had appeared at my side when I heard her soft voice.

"Nacchan."

Normally, I would jolt in surprise, but I was able to keep my cool as I slowly turned to look at her.

"Where did this picture come from?" I asked. I hadn't seen it the last time I was in this room.

"My friend made it for me some time ago. I used to have it hanging in the office on the second floor, but I don't use the office much anymore, so I decided to bring it down here."

Now that I thought about it, I had never asked what kind of job she'd had. Although I thought about it now, I was more interested in the painting.

"How could anyone actually draw a picture like this?"

My question was not one of suspicion. Although I would only come to learn it later, there was a word for what I was feeling: admiration.

"You have some really talented friends," I said.

I really did attribute this to talent. I would never be able to draw a picture so splendid, no matter how long I practiced. I could more readily imagine myself a princess or a CEO. Only a person with special hands could create such a magical picture.

Granny, however, shook her head. "It's not just talent. There aren't that many people as talented as the man who painted this, but there *are* others."

"No way."

I couldn't believe it. There were multiple people in this world who could make pictures like this? That was more shocking than if she had told me there were sorcerers among us.

"There are more talented people out there than you think. However, it takes more than just talent to paint a picture like this."

"What does it take, then? Effort?"

"Of course, but there's something even more important than that. I've never known anyone who loved drawing more than the man who painted this. I've lived far longer than you and I've met many people, but not once did I ever meet anyone who had art on his mind more than him."

"So it takes love to make a picture like this?"

"Yes. Only someone who gives their all could make something so truly amazing."

Although I cannot remember it, that must have been why I was so moved by Minami-san's story, I thought. Then it occurred to me that there was someone I wished to ask about.

"People who are talented and love what they do shouldn't be embarrassed about it."

"You had a friend like that, didn't you?"

"He's not my friend. But he does draw. He seems really embarrassed about it, though. Hey, Granny, what is the person who drew that picture doing now?"

"He's living in another country with his family."

"I see. For some reason I thought he might've been your lover."

I was still unable to take my eyes off of the painting, so I have no idea how she seemed then, but I could tell by her tone that she was enjoying talking with me.

"And why is that?"

"Because it says 'love' right here."

I pointed to the right-hand corner of the picture. I could not read English, but I could decipher that much at least. The English word that was written there, I was certain, was "love."

However...

"Hee, Nacchan, that doesn't say 'love.' Love is spelled ell-oh-vee-ee. This is ell-*eye*-vee-ee. It's pronounced 'live.'"

I got as close as I could to the picture and, surely enough, *Live* was written there. Also, although I did not know the meaning, were the letters *em-ee*.

"*Live*...what?"

"*Live Me. Me* means yourself. Together it means 'Let me live,' though actually the grammar is wrong. It's the artist's signature. A bit of a joke."

Not knowing English, I did not get the joke. I could only tilt my head.

"Life really is like a diet."

"You get results through effort?"

"No, things aren't any fun when you're too dense. Not when it comes to fashion or jokes."

"I see!"

"Yep. So I need to get smarter."

"You will. Now then, let's do something that's just as important as studying. Can I ask you to do a job for me?"

"A job? What is it?" I asked.

She smiled at me devilishly and held something up. My face lit up with joy—I knew exactly what it was for.

"Shave me some ice. In summer, eating shaved ice is an important as doing homework, isn't it?"

"Absolutely!"

Apparently, she had been up on the second floor, searching for the shaved ice machine. It was no wonder I had been unable to find her.

With the smell of that wonderful drawing still lingering in my nostrils, we decided to move to the cool living room and make our shaved ice there. We retrieved a square-shaped block from the bottom shelf of Granny's freezer, and I shaved with all my might. Granny prepared the syrup and spoons, while Miss Bobtail circled around in amusement, as though she had never seen shaved ice before. Finally, she plopped down on her behind, looking around.

I poured bright red syrup onto the mountain of fresh, snowy ice. I loved every flavor, but today I felt like strawberry. Granny seemed to be of the same mind, and the two of us ate together, dyeing our tongues red. As for my golden-eyed friend, although I had gone to the trouble of pouring syrup for her too, she only seemed to be interested in the parts without it, and so I shaved some more off the block onto a plate. Soon, she was happily licking the heap, lost in her own satisfaction. Perhaps she merely wished to avoid staining her little tongue.

As we ate our ice, I told Granny all about everything that had been happening, including what Skank-san had told me. I thought that Granny might be able to give me some answer, but she only said the same thing as Skank-san.

"Hmm, well, let's see... I think this really is something that you have to think about on your own."

"I know that. That's why I came to ask you for a hint."

"A hint, hm?"

Granny sipped the tea she had prepared to settle her stomach. I thought about it, wondering what sort of hint I should ask for. Meanwhile, my sun-basking friend lay beside me, thinking of nothing at all.

"Say, Granny. Your friend, the one who painted that picture. What kind of person was he?"

"Hm?"

"My classmate, the one who hasn't been coming to school? He likes drawing pictures, too. I figured you might know a lot about people who draw."

"I see." She smiled, even more warmly than Skank-san. "Like other artists, this friend of mine was an incredibly delicate person. Artists hurt easily, and are weaker than others in many ways."

"I know plenty about that."

"But they are also kinder and more pure than almost anyone else. People who make art can see the world clearly. The good and the bad things come to them more directly than to anyone else. The pictures they draw aren't like photos. When you look at them, you see how the world looks to them."

I tried thinking of the pictures I had seen in my life, and of Kiriyuu-kun's drawings. They were like magic. I certainly did not see the world that way. Still, if the painting in Granny's bedroom reflected the true shape of the world, then the world might truly be a beautiful place.

"There could never be pain or sadness in such a beautiful world," I said.

"Yes, that's true. And yet, there are pain and sadness in *this* world, aren't there? In truth, such places could never exist in our world. Artists know that. That what is why they feel pain and hurt so much more strongly."

I thought of Kiriyuu-kun's face when he was being ridiculed. Somehow or other, I think I understood just what Granny was saying.

"Even if that wasn't true, it's only human nature that the bad things linger in our hearts longer than the good."

Indeed, what I witnessed at the supermarket and the sight of Kiriyuu's eyes were etched deeply into my heart, more so than all the wonderful things that had happened in the days since.

Then I thought of Minami-san's tears. "Is it the same for people who write stories?"

"Yes, probably. However, I think that people who draw are even lonelier than people who write. Stories are made of words, aren't they? Words are far easier to convey than images."

"I think I'll go for the stories, then. I want to be able to share what's in my heart directly... Yep, there's no other path for me."

As I stood up, holding my shaved ice dish and filled with determination, Granny gave an elegant laugh. "Did you find something?"

"Yeah. I promised Hitomi-sensei that I'd be the ally of that cowardly artist. First off, I've got to tell him that."

"If that's your decision, then I approve. However, there's a chance that boy might be less cowardly than you think."

"Hitomi-sensei said the same thing. He really is a coward, though. Spineless, too. He can't even say how he feels."

And yet, when he looked at me, I felt like his eyes were conveying his true emotions.

That evening, after I returned home from Granny's, I could not get Kiriyuu-kun off my mind, even as I ate dinner, brushed my teeth, and climbed into bed. There's no way to know everything about someone else, so you have to think about it. But no matter how hard I thought, all I could think of was our differences. I could not find one single way in which we were the same, as Skank-san had implied.

Besides, there was still one thing that I desperately needed to consider: How should I tell him that I was his ally? By letter? By phone? I couldn't text him, since I did not have a cell phone.

And so...

Chapter 7

THE NEXT DAY, after morning announcements, I called after Hitomi-sensei and presented her with the decision I had made the night before. "I'll take the handouts over to Kiriyuu-kun's house for you today. There's something that I need to tell him."

She appeared troubled at this proposal. That made sense—she assumed I was part of the reason that Kiriyuu had stopped coming to school. Although she wouldn't say it, I knew that was true.

"You said I should be his ally, didn't you? An ally of justice should never stop being an ally just because someone won't come to them. They go to the aid of the weak."

I refrained from adding "Obviously the idiots in our class are the bad guys."

But Hitomi-sensei still appeared troubled. I began thinking about what I ought to do should my proposal be rejected, and thought I would just go to Kiriyuu-kun's house anyway. After all, Hitomi-sensei had said herself that adults were not always correct.

Of course, that did not mean that I was any more correct, just because I was a child. I knew that the decision Hitomi-sensei had come to meant she had decided to have faith in me.

"All right. You can take the handouts today."

"I will honor that duty!"

"Good, but I'd like you to promise me three things."

She made a serious face and held up three fingers. It was the sort of serious face that I loved on her. I was sure that she was thinking of both me and Kiriyuu-kun from the bottom of her heart.

"First, if you manage to see Kiriyuu-kun, I want you to tell him that I will always be waiting for him."

I was stunned. "You haven't seen him?"

"No, he still hasn't wanted to see me."

"He really is completely spineless."

As I said this, she folded down a second finger. "That's number two. You mustn't go after him. Attacking someone is not part of being their ally. So you absolutely must not try to force him to come to school."

This made sense to me. It was the duty of an ally of justice to scold naughty children, and although Kiriyuu-kun was spineless, he was not naughty. And so, I could not attack him.

"And the last one?"

"Third, you have to promise not to call your classmates bad. Everyone is just as worried about Kiriyuu-kun as you are."

I heard this, and I thought: *She really* is *off the mark.*

I wonder if she realized that the last promise was the only one that I did not nod to. When I returned to the classroom, I looked over the kids who were causing a ruckus. Everyone was passing the time as they always did, the usual vapid looks on their faces, as though Kiriyuu-kun had never even been part of the class. No one else said anything about Kiriyuu or asked Hitomi-sensei about him. Not a single one. And so, her third request was a lie. An absolute falsehood.

I had no idea if this was a happy thing or a sad thing, but it soon became clear that day that I, although I was only a child, was not confused or mistaken.

At break, something occurred that left me speechless.

"What? Why would you do somethin' like that for a thief's kid? Do you like him or something?"

I was copying my notes onto a sheet of paper when this idiot boy spoke up, his stupid face pulled into a grin. Just as he had suggested, I was doing this for Kiriyuu-kun. *If I am going to his house anyway, I might as well share the lesson with him in my nice, neat handwriting,* I thought.

I somehow managed to pull my cutting words back into my mouth, sighed, and answered his question. "Yes, I do like him, at least more than I like you all. He's a weakling, but he's great at drawing."

"He's weak because he's always drawin.'"

That might be true, I thought, recalling what Granny had said, but I could not allow an idiot to hurt others simply because they said one thing with some truth to it. I ignored him and continued copying my notes.

The idiot made a face, as though his nonexistent pride had been hurt. "Don't ignore me!"

When I continued to do just that, he snatched away the paper I had been copying and raised his arm, holding it up for the class to see.

"She's in love with Kiriyuu!" he shouted.

Everyone in the classroom turned our way, muttering. The idiot looked at me, his eyes burning with a victorious pride, as if he had somehow claimed a victory. How utterly revolting. I heaved a deep sigh and prepared to teach this boy the depths of his own idiocy.

"I know you're excited to show the class just how stupid you are, so give it back already."

I stood to take the paper from his hand, but he twisted, holding it away from me. Anyone who looked at this scene would have been able to tell at a glance which of us was in the wrong. Any one of them could have persuaded him to give the paper back. One of the kids behind him could have just taken it from him and given it back themselves.

However, no one did any such thing. Even though they all knew that Kiriyuu-kun was away, and that I was always fighting on his behalf, they did nothing. That was how I knew that Hitomi-sensei had lied.

I sighed and asked the idiot, "You won't give it back?"

The boy ignored me. I had promised Hitomi-sensei. I would not attack my allies.

"Since you won't give it back, I guess that makes you a thief."

136

In other words, it was fine to attack an enemy.

The idiot glared at me, his face going bright red.

"You know what 'thief' means, don't you? You must, given how many times you've said it. A thief is someone who takes something that belongs to someone else without asking, right? Then I guess you're a thief, too. And while I don't know if Kiriyuu-kun's father really did steal something, since I didn't see it happen, I know for sure that you are a thief. See, right there, you took something of mine, didn't you?"

His face grew redder and redder. At this rate I thought he might just explode. However, I was not finished. If he did explode, I would just have to apologize.

"Stealing is bad, isn't it?" I said. "You attacked Kiriyuu-kun because you think so too, right? In that case, let's go along with what you were saying before. If Kiriyuu-kun's father being a thief makes him a thief too, then I guess that makes *everyone* in your family thieves! What a dreadful family! Your mother, your father, everyone, all thieves. Maybe even your grandma and grandpa, too? If just being associated with someone bad makes you bad too, then maybe your friends are all thieves! No wait, I wonder if just being in the same room as you would make someone a thief? Then I guess maybe I'm a thief now too. That really sucks. I'm not like you."

"*Shut up!*"

The moment the boy's shrill voice reached my ears, something else happened. I saw the boy falling away from me. No, it was me who was falling. I could see the ceiling above me. It took a moment to realize what was happening. I sat there, dumbfounded, as the pain of the blow reached my brain. My chair fell down on its side as well. Perhaps I had pulled it with me.

Anyone who saw this would know right away: this was assault. Violence. Something we were taught never to do.

As I stood up, thinking to admonish him, something struck me softly in the head. I picked it up and spread it out, only to find that it was the paper I had been using to copy notes for Kiriyuu-kun.

"Everyone hates you," said the boy.

He had taken something from me, destroyed it, and even physically attacked me. On top of all that, he was insulting me. If anyone could watch over this scene and say I was the one in the wrong, they were crazy. *Surely someone will come to my aid,* I thought.

And yet, though they had been sitting there the whole time, not a single person stepped up to offer their hand or comfort me.

What Hitomi-sensei had said really was a lie. And so I, who always spoke my mind, said precisely what I was thinking, loud enough that everyone could hear.

"You're all thieves."

As though to stop the reverberating of my words, the bell rang, signaling the end of break.

After afternoon announcements, with the handouts for Kiriyuu in hand, I headed straight out of the building, not stopping to receive a candy from Shintarou-sensei, who sat beside

Hitomi-sensei in the faculty room. I did not offer a single word of greeting to any of my classmates as I passed them. Instead, I met up with my furry friend near my home, then headed to Kiriyuu-kun's house.

I knew where he lived already. I had run into him along the street before. Once I was in the general area, I just had to look at the nameplates.

Among the rows of identical single-family homes, there was only one with "Kiriyuu" written in front of it. I remembered how the surname was written in kanji, because I had previously remarked on how cool it looked.

"Koyanagi is cooler, though," I said to myself, pressing the doorbell of the house.

I waited for about a minute, but it did not seem as though anyone was coming. I pressed it a second time, but got the same result.

I could not imagine that Kiriyuu-kun was out. Even I, when I stayed home sick, refused to go out—not wanting to run into the people who were still going to school. Kiriyuu-kun certainly did not have the courage.

Maybe he didn't want to see me. I pressed the button a third time, considering how I ought to spend the next minute, when finally a voice came from the speaker connected to the doorbell.

"*Hello...?*"

Although the voice had little life to it, I could tell it was Kiriyuu-kun's mother, having heard her speak on class observation day.

"Good afternoon! I'm Kiriyuu-kun's classmate. I came to bring him some handouts!"

"Ah...thank you, just a moment."

I waited obediently, and soon Kiriyuu-kun's mother opened the front door.

"Wait here a minute," I told my little friend, sitting at my feet and licking her fur.

I bowed my head to the woman.

"Good afternoon!"

"You're Koyanagi-san, right? The one who sits next to Hikari."

Although I had never spoken to her before, she seemed to know who I was. I wasn't sure why that would be, but I was glad. Hikari was Kiriyuu-kun's given name. Kiriyuu Hikari. Such an impressive name for someone like him.

"Usually, Hitomi-sensei brings these, but I guess that was your job today. Thank you."

"Yes, I asked her to. I have some business with Kiriyuu-kun."

Hearing the word "business," Kiriyuu's mother made the same face that Hitomi-sensei had that morning. She was troubled. Perhaps even she thought it was my fault that Kiriyuu-kun hadn't been coming to school, even though this was the first time I had ever spoken to her.

"Business?" she asked.

I gave an honest response. If you want someone to believe you, you can only give them the truth. "I came to tell him that I'm his ally, and that I want him to come back to school. If he doesn't, then I won't have anyone to pair up with during class."

I could tell that she let her guard down a little. Sure enough, telling the truth was the only way to go—honest people get results. She smiled. "Come on in."

It was the first time I had been inside his house. The smells of cooking and laundry permeated the whole building, so much stronger than in mine. That was probably because people were only in my home from night until morning. A while ago, I might even have been jealous.

I was led to the living room, where I sat on the sofa and drank the orange juice she gave me. It was reason enough to be glad I'd come. Orange juice was sweet and delicious. As I drank it, I asked Kiriyuu's mother about something that had bothered me since I'd entered the house.

"Where's Kiriyuu-kun? Did he go out?" I asked,

She shook her head, sipping her coffee. "Hikari is in his room upstairs. He spends most of his time shut up in there."

"I wonder if he's drawing."

I had merely said what I was thinking, but Kiriyuu's mother looked surprised.

"Oh? You know about his drawing, then? He's always hiding it."

"He always hides it at school, too. He's so good at it though, he should show it off more. I think his drawings are beautiful."

If there was a moment when I fully won over Kiriyuu's mother, that was it. There really was nothing to be gained from telling lies.

"If Kiriyuu-kun has been locking himself up in his room drawing this whole time, then he has my support and I can't wait to see. But I can't support him in hiding something that he likes."

"Tell that to Hikari. You really are his ally, Koyanagi-san."

"Yes, I have never once been his enemy."

I finished my orange juice and climbed the stairs to the second floor, led by Kiriyuu's mother, who was still smiling. There was a brightly lit hallway on the second floor with a number of doors, none with any defining characteristics. We came to a stop before one of them. It was a subdued door, not plastered up with pictures as mine was.

Kiriyuu's mother knocked. "Hikari, there's a friend here to see you."

We weren't friends, but I was busy listening for the response from behind the door and did not bother to say this. A short time passed before there was any reply.

"Who is it...?"

The voice was very weak. Anyone who didn't know Kiriyuu-kun would probably think that he was sick. However, knowing him from all our time in the classroom, I did not think it differed from his normal voice in the slightest.

Before his mother could say my name, I took a step closer. "It's me."

I could tell right away that he recognized me. I heard a scrambling sound from within. What was he so frantic about? I wasn't like those idiots who picked on him.

"*Why...?*" he asked.

The question sounded as though it came from the bottom of his heart.

"I brought you your handouts. And I copied my class notes for you."

"Hitomi-sensei didn't come...to bring those?"

"I came instead. I'm the one who copied the notes over. Plus, there's something I want to tell you." Kiriyuu-kun gave no reply. And so, I continued. "Listen, Kiriyuu-kun. I'm your ally. I've never once been your enemy. So, you can come to school at ease."

Still he said nothing.

"You might've gotten the wrong impression, but I really am your ally. If anything happens, me and Hitomi-sensei will both fight for you. But you have to fight, too. Life is like the first runner in a relay. If you don't start moving, the race won't ever begin."

Predictably, he stayed silent.

"That's what I came to tell you today."

I don't know if I was able to get across everything that I wanted to say, but I had at least said the most important thing. I fell quiet and waited for his reply.

That waiting seemed to stretch on forever. Thankfully, before I could grow any older, his reply finally came. However, it was one I could not accept.

"Go home..."

I was stunned. His next words came flying out like an attack.

"Don't come back. I'm not going to school anymore."

What shocked me was not only the meaning of his words, but the scent of his voice, which was the same scent I had gotten when he glared at me in the classroom.

I was utterly lost. Kiriyuu's mother probably was as well. Unthinking, I put my hand on the door.

"Why?"

"I'm not going to fight."

It was those words. Those words were the wrong ones. Those words lit a horrible flame in my heart. The spark of what happened that afternoon was still burning, and it now blazed in the wrong direction. I had already forgotten that his mother was standing behind me.

"If you don't fight, people are going to keep making fun of you."

Silence.

"About your drawing, and your father."

Silence still.

"You haven't done anything wrong! People are all wrong about you! You have to fight!"

I was frustrated. Frustrated by the fact that Kiriyuu-kun was being ridiculed, that he would not fight for himself, and that there was nothing I could do about it.

"No," Kiriyuu-kun said softly. "I'm not strong like you."

"You...*coward!!!*"

My voice came out so loud. I must have sucked in so much air that I was surprised the people around me didn't suffocate. I was shocked by my own voice, but more than that...

"*Go home!*"

I had heard Kiriyuu-kun shout before, so this was not what surprised me.

"I hate them! I hate all of them! But I hate *you* the most!"

I was sure that he was crying, though I did not know what about. Normally, I would have said something like "I thought that men didn't cry," but I was too shocked. I was shocked that he was hurt, and at how black my own heart became at those words.

I could not stay here any longer. Although I knew it was rude, I shoved the notes from my backpack into Kiriyuu's mother's hands and fled the house.

I even ignored my faithful friend as I left, rushing to sit down on a bench at the edge of a park. And then, before my little friend's curious eyes, I wept.

I did not go to see Skank-san or Granny that day. I still had plenty of time until curfew, but I couldn't possibly go to see them with tears in my eyes.

I had that
same
Dream
again

Chapter 8

THE NEXT DAY, Kiriyuu-kun did not come to school, just as he had said. Somehow I managed to drag myself there, the blackness still lingering in my heart. I couldn't possibly skip school after being so adamant that Kiriyuu should come. And yet, he did not show.

I prayed that the darkness inside my body would leave, but it was not going anywhere. Of course, I wanted to go back home. I wanted to hurry up and see my friends. That was my only wish. I wanted to see Skank-san, and Granny, and Miss Bobtail.

Come to think of it, where *had* Minami-san gone?

As I thought about my missing friend during social studies, I found myself on the verge of tears again. I decided to go to the library during break. There, the smell of the books and the treasures concealed within were sure to give me some comfort.

This plan was at least mildly successful. The darkness still remained within me, but at least its rampaging was contained and I managed to keep my tears held back.

I could at least keep the wicked thing at bay until after school. That way, I could eat ice cream with Skank-san like always, and go to Granny's to eat sweets. It would be best if I could simply forget about Kiriyuu; if I could forget about all the unpleasant things.

Such was my way of thinking. And yet I could not think that way for long. I had to find a better way to clear this gloomy shroud from my heart.

It was as I was leaving the library that I saw him, walking a bit ahead of me down the hall. I approached him from behind and called out.

"Salutations, Ogiwara-kun."

His shoulders trembled, as though my greeting had surprised him. While waiting for him to turn around, I thought about what I was going to say. *I've been reading* Our Seven Days' War *lately. What have you been reading, Ogiwara-kun?*

If there was still one person in our class who didn't hate me, even if he was the only one, then that would lighten the load on my heart. I prayed only for that. And yet, life is like a fever when you're sick: it's usually worse than you imagine.

I had called Ogiwara-kun's name. And yet, he showed no signs of turning to meet me. Worse, he began walking faster towards the classroom.

Thinking that perhaps he hadn't heard me, or that he was surprised about something else, I called out to him once more.

"Hey, Ogiwara-kun."

He did not reply, nor did he stop. It was odd. I called to him one more time.

"Ogiwara-kun?"

Sure enough, he did not turn. I called his name again and again, each time my voice growing louder. By the time we reached the classroom, my voice was as loud as it had been yesterday with Kiriyuu-kun.

"Ogiwara-kun!"

Without a reply, Ogiwara took his seat and opened his textbook. I only had a vague idea of what was going on, but I didn't want to acknowledge it. However, I knew from the way that the boys of my class grinned, with dirty looks upon their faces, that my wish was not going to come true.

Ignoring someone. The most foolish, idiotic form of bullying.

Until then, I had not thought to worry myself so much over it. Now, however, my heart was taken by a darkness that grew even hungrier. My heart was consumed by the knowledge that even I could be bullied, and even Ogiwara-kun could participate in it.

I only learned far later that it was Ogiwara-kun who spread the rumors about Kiriyuu-kun's father. None of that would have mattered to me in that moment, though. In that moment, my mind was in disarray. I was devastated that Ogiwara-kun had betrayed me. That the whole world had.

I don't remember any of the time that passed between that moment and when I arrived at Skank-san's home that afternoon.

When I finally snapped back to reality, I was ringing Skank-san's doorbell. I could not recall how I had gotten there. Miss

Bobtail was not present. Before I knew it, my finger was simply on the bell.

"Coming," said Skank-san's sleepy, warm voice from within.

The door cracked open, and Skank-san's sleepy face peered out. When she saw my face, she invited me in without another word.

I shed my shoes, entering the room and shuffling to the corner. I huddled up there, my face buried. She had already seen me plainly, but wearing a pitiful face wasn't clever-seeming at all, and so I pulled myself into a little human triangle.

Even as she came back into the room, Skank-san didn't ask about it. I heard the sound of her opening the refrigerator and placing something atop the table near me.

"I found this while I was out today and I thought it was unusual, so I bought some. Eat up."

I shook my head, not even looking up to see what it was. It made a swishing sound as my forehead rubbed against the fabric of my skirt.

I heard her stand up again, and the smell of coffee wafted over—two of my favorite things. However, I was in no mood for it today.

Perhaps she is annoyed, even angry, I thought. Here was this horribly rude child who suddenly burst into her house crying, and wouldn't even say a thing.

She finished making her coffee and returned to where she had been sitting. All I could hear was the sound of the air conditioner. Even that only lasted a short while. Soon after, I heard another sound.

"Happiness won't cooome, wandering my way, sooo thaaat's why I set ooout to find it todaaay!"

I heard Skank-san's beautiful singing voice reaching both heights and depths that I could not yet reach myself. Like a picture painted up in shifting reds and blues.

She is probably trying to get me to cheer up, I thought, but I could not sing.

Her singing stopped on a dime.

"What is happiness?" she asked suddenly.

I was sure she could see my ears prick up at this. I buried my face deeper into my knees, but she continued talking.

"I've been thinking about it ever since you first asked."

"…"

"I just figured out the answer today."

I lifted my head, but just as I was about to meet her eyes, I flopped back down again. There was the wonderful smell of her coffee (despite its bitter taste), and the gaudy scent of her perfume and makeup. I was intrigued to hear Skank-san's answer.

Because the room was so quiet, she could probably tell that my interest had been piqued. She gulped down a mouthful of coffee.

"Now, this is just my answer, so it's probably different from yours. But it might give you some hint, so I thought I would share it with you." She did not wait for me to acknowledge her. "Happiness is being able to think seriously about someone."

"…"

"I went shopping today. I bought food for breakfast tomorrow, and drinks, and a new bottle of shampoo. It was a normal, everyday task, something I do every single day, nothing special at all. As I bought my bread and milk, I thought about whether I had forgotten to buy anything. It occurred to me that you might be coming over today, and that I should buy something sweet. I tried to remember what we'd eaten together before, what we might eat together today, and how I hoped it would make you happy. Before I knew it, I was thinking about nothing but you."

I remained quiet, and she continued.

"When I realized this, I was surprised. I had never thought that seriously about anyone, not in a long time. There was never anyone who I wanted to make happy, who I wanted to spend time with. I had given up on all that. It had been so long, I'd forgotten just how full your heart could be when you give all your thoughts to someone."

"..."

"You know something, little miss? I've grown into an adult who just gives up on things that I don't like, or things that are painful. I was able to fake it before, but I wasn't happy. I had already forgotten the shape of happiness. But, today, I finally remembered it."

"..."

"I've remembered the shape of happiness, all thanks to you. Thank you."

I could tell that she had stood up. The floorboards creaked here and there. As she moved, it made a sound like a mouse's cry. The squeaking sound drew nearer and nearer, and then it stopped. Skank-san sat down beside me, close enough for me to feel her gentle warmth.

"That's the end of my babbling. Thank you for listening," she said. "I know that listening to adults can be boring. That's just like you, though, to be able to sit and listen so quietly. All right, here's your reward for paying attention to my boring story."

She wrapped her pretty fingers around my hands.

"As thanks, if there's ever anything that you want to talk about, I will always listen for as long as you like."

I might just cry again, I thought, but I didn't.

Her words had made me happy. They overflowed with kindness, but they were not coddling. *I really do hope that I grow into an adult like her someday,* I thought. *Plus, she said that she's found happiness thanks to me. There no greater joy than that.*

It would have been nice if I could jump for joy now, but I could not. I couldn't believe in her idea of happiness.

I spoke in my crumpled voice for the first time that afternoon. "I thought about it."

"Hm?"

"I thought really hard! But it was pointless!" It wasn't right to shout at Skank-san so loudly. I took a breath. "I'm sorry."

But aside from my loud voice, I could not apologize for my reaction.

"I thought long, and I thought hard about it. I thought about it *day and night*. I thought about it, just like you said! I thought about my classmate harder than I ever thought about anything, but all it did was get me ignored! He said that he hated me! That isn't happiness."

"I see..."

"I'm done thinking about other people."

"Don't say that."

Her words were scolding, like a schoolteacher's. Adults were always saying that friendship was the most important thing in this world. She was probably angry at me for saying something so out of line. I was disappointed in myself. That was not what friends did. However, the next thing she did assured me that I was not being scolded.

She squeezed my hands. And then, in a quiet voice that seemed to hold back a world of sorrow, she said, "You'll end up like me."

I don't know why there was such unconcealed sadness buried in her voice.

"So you mustn't think like that."

"Why not?"

My question came from the bottom of my heart. *Skank-san is such a wonderful person,* I thought. I wished that all adults were like her. No, I wished that all *people* could be as wonderful as her. If so, we would have a world where everyone was clever, with a wonderful smell. A world so beautiful it could not even be drawn in pictures.

"I want to be an adult just like you. If I was as smart, and nice, and wonderful as you, I wouldn't need any friends at school."

I squeezed her hands back. As I did, she let out a slow, quiet sigh that I did not understand. It was so quiet that I could hear the air conditioner again.

"There's a dream I have often. I had that same dream again this morning."

"What...kind of dream?"

"I dream about a girl. This girl is smart and reads tons of books and knows a lot of things, which makes her think that she's a very special person. Different from everyone around her."

Was this a story? Before I could ask, she continued.

"It's important to think that you're special. However, this girl is mistaken in her thinking. She thinks that everyone else around her is stupid. Although this isn't true at all, because this girl's cleverness is what makes her special, she thinks that being clever is the *only* path to becoming special. She thinks that as long as you have that, you can become someone important."

She gave a little cough.

"This girl is an important child, but someone who belittles others will never be liked by anyone. She becomes more and more hated by the people around her. The worst part is, this girl thinks that that's just fine, because she hates all the idiot children around her. Well...now that I think about it, she doesn't really hate them. It's just that she can't seem to think about any of them."

She gripped my hands.

"There are probably people who try to understand this girl, but this girl grows older and older, not giving a thought to anyone. She's locked up in her own little world, devoting her time to growing smarter. She believes that as long as she does that, one day she'll be happy. But she's wrong."

I gripped her hands back.

"By the time she's an adult, this girl is very smart. But that's all that she has. One day, she realizes that there's nothing else around her. She should have become an important person, but she realizes that there's no one around to praise her."

This sounds just like...

I suddenly became very worried for this girl. "What happens to her?"

"I can tell you the rest of the story from here, but I'm not sure that you would understand. Even if you did, I can't tell you what it means. I don't want to. Do you still want to hear it?"

I nodded, my face still buried in my knees.

"Okay, well, this girl begins to think that her life has no meaning. Then she starts to think that nothing matters, and begins abusing her body, and mistreating her own heart. She goes to dangerous places, gets into dangerous things, and suffers dangers to herself. Still, she's not unhappy about this. It feels good to destroy herself. Although her life is something that she built for herself, she hates it. She ruins and ruins and ruins, but she still needs money, so she neglects her own well-being in order to earn it. Before she knows it, she finds herself dwelling in that place. Of course, even down there, there are proud and wonderful people. The circumstances and the job itself aren't at fault. That girl is the bad one here. And surely enough, more and more ruin is visited upon this prideless girl every day. But humans can get used to anything. Once she grows used to it, she realizes one more thing: there is no point in destroying herself, either. And so she thinks that she may as well put an end to this life."

I was quiet.

Just as she said, I did not understand the meaning of her story. I could imagine, but only vaguely, and I had no idea what she meant by "dangerous things" or "mistreating her heart." There was only one thing that I was certain of. "That girl is you, isn't she?"

Skank-san was silent.

"What does 'putting an end to a life' mean?" I asked, worried about this girl's future.

"Who knows?" Skank-san said. "In the end, she doesn't end her life, so I don't know what that would have meant. On the day when she thinks of ending it, a visitor suddenly shows up at her home. It's a little girl, carrying a little friend with her."

I finally lifted my head and looked at her. I gave her a clear look at my face, messy with snot and tears. I don't know why I did that. I guess I just wanted to look at her face. She was smiling at me kindly, as she always did.

"From there on out, her days are so much fun. She didn't have any friends before that, but she realizes how much better things could have been if only she had learned to love someone sooner. But you can never take back the past."

You can't get back time. I remembered Minami-san saying that.

"I'm excited to see what kind of person you grow into, but I'm worried about you. Do you know why?"

I shook my head.

"Because you're just like that little girl. You can't let yourself walk the same path. You have to find happiness. That's why you can't talk about disconnecting from everyone."

As I thought about what she was saying, I squeezed her hand again.

I was so confused. I felt as though I was trapped in the middle of a labyrinth.

Because I was clever, I understood what she meant. But understanding what she meant and being able to follow through were two wholly different things. I had already decided that I wished to have nothing more to do with the people who had hurt me, after all. Plus, even if I could change my thinking, I still didn't think that anyone besides Skank-san and Granny would want to be near me. Even Ogiwara-kun and Kiriyuu-kun hated me. There was no hope.

I suddenly wanted to hear more about this girl, who was so much like me. "That girl liked books, right?"

"Mm, yes, just like you. She loved books, and she was always reading. She once thought that she might become someone who wrote stories herself, but when she realized there was no one around her to read them, she forgot that dream."

"What about her mother and father?"

"I'm sure that they're still living happily together somewhere. She hasn't seen them in a long time. Once, she thought that she'd go back home, and went all the way to her old house, but she couldn't ring the doorbell. She was too afraid."

"She didn't have any friends to talk about books with, or friends to eat ice cream with, or friends with short tails?"

"Nope, none. And so, there was no one to tell her when she was wrong."

"Did she have any favorite phrases, like me?"

She answered my flood of insolent questions directly, one after the other. This made me happy, and so I piled on more questions.

"Phrases?"

She stared out the window, as if digging for some day back in her memory. My eyes were trained on her face. She put her fingers to her chin and thought about it.

"Phrases, yeah, there was something she was always saying. So much so that I wonder why I forgot about it. Her catchphrase was...wait...hm?"

She eyes turned from the window back to me, her eyelids fluttering. Then, she stopped blinking and her eyes opened so wide I thought they might just go flying off.

"What's wrong?"

"My...catchphrase when I was little. It was: 'Life is like...'"

Perhaps because she was so shocked, she had forgotten to refer to herself as "this girl," which seemed to be the whole conceit of the game. I was shocked, too.

"That's the same as me!"

"When I was a child," she said, her lips trembling. "I loved the comic 'Peanuts.' I read the Japanese translation all the time, and there was something that the main character, Charlie Brown, said. 'Life is like an ice cream cone...'"

"You have to learn to lick it..."

"That's right! Did you read them?"

I shook my head fervently. "I love that quote, too! It's a really clever joke."

"This must be kismet..."

Kismet, she had said. Not "fate," or "destiny," which I thought was wonderful of her. I knew the kanji for kismet: *en*. The fact that it so closely resembled the kanji for *midori,* green, reminded me of the mysteriousness of life. The living things that died and became the earth, and the green grasses that grew from them, upon which other living things would graze. In which case, the fact that she and I had met truly was kismet.

I put my hands together in thanks for such a word.

Although I didn't say anything, she seemed to share my feelings. She grinned, wrapping her hands around mine. "You see? You can't abandon your connections to everyone. When you open your heart, you open yourself to wonderful encounters, just like this."

Perhaps that's true, I thought.

"It might be too late," she went on. "But if such things can happen, then maybe I can try again, just one more time."

Apparently, she had completely given up on talking about "that girl."

"You have so many wonderful encounters waiting on you, little miss," she said. "So many more than me. As long as you don't give up on other people, then I'm sure you'll lead a happy life."

"Really...?"

"Yeah, really."

If she said it was true, then it must be. I loved Skank-san, and I believed in her. Hitomi-sensei had taught me that sometimes adults spoke the truth. *If the day ever comes that I can escape this darkness inside me,* I thought, *and come to like someone, perhaps even my classmates, then there might just be a happy life out there.*

And yet...

"But...there's no one who I can get along with anymore."

"That's not true. What about that classmate of yours, the one who likes books?"

I thought of Ogiwara-kun's face, but as I did, the blackness seemed to creep back into my heart. "He ignored me."

"I see. I *was* wondering if he was the one who said that he hated you."

"He wasn't. It was the other boy I was talking about before, the one who won't come to school. I went to his house. I wanted to tell him that I was his ally, but he was way more spineless than I thought. When I told him that, he said that he hated me the most, even more than those creeps at school."

"Well...that *was* your fault."

Hearing these words, I completely forgot what I had been about to say. *How? How was I in the wrong? I was trying to help him,* I thought, but I could not voice the words. I don't know whether Skank-san understood this, but she stroked my hair.

"And it was my fault, too. I was wrong about the hint I gave you. You're clever, but you're just like me. You aren't so clever when it comes to connecting with people."

She gave an eerie giggle, but I couldn't be unhappy to hear that I was the same as her.

In that case, maybe Skank-san can teach a blockhead like me a thing or two, I thought.

"Say, little miss," she asked. "Are there any foods that you hate in your school lunch?"

I had no idea why she would ask me such a question at a time like this, but I would never ignore her questions.

"I hate natto. It smells weird."

"Yeah, I hated it too."

"But you can't leave any food on your plate."

"That's right. It's good for your health, so you better eat that natto up. So then, how would you feel if, just as you were working up the courage to eat that natto, your teacher came and shouted at you, 'You eat that natto *right now!*'?"

"My teacher would never do that, but I wouldn't like it. I'd probably get mad, and then I really wouldn't want to eat that natto."

She gave a big nod.

"Well, you did the exact same thing to that boy who didn't want to come to school, didn't you?"

I had never experienced it, nor had I ever heard anyone even talk about it, but I felt as though I had just been struck by lightning. In fact, I was sure of it. It was a harsher blow than when I had struck my head against a wall, and prickled more than my limbs after sitting seiza for far too long on my Shichi-Go-San Day. The darkness began to inch out of my heart with a crackling sound.

"Oh, I see." I realized that I had stepped out of line. "He probably was trying to fight."

"Yes, probably. Maybe he really is spineless, but in that case, you shouldn't get mad at him. That boy had something to tell you. He wasn't ignoring you."

Skank-san really was far sharper than me. Again, I had not even considered this fact. I already had the idea that Kiriyuu-kun was spineless, that he was a coward, incapable of fighting. And yet, maybe he had been trying to fight, in his own small way.

"Besides, there are other ways to fight. Maybe his way was just to bear it and keep on drawing, so that he could show all those other people someday."

Of course. No matter how much people made fun of him, no matter how much he hid it, he never once seemed to think of giving up drawing.

"His way of fighting might be different from yours, but deep down, the two of you are the same. I am, too. There are things that bother you, that make you sad. You hate those things, and you hope to have allies on your side. I'm sure he regrets saying that he hated you. You're smarter than the other children, but they think a lot about things, too."

It was the same hint that she had given me before. *Everyone is different, but we're all the same.*

"So, what should we do?"

"Think about what you wish someone would do when you're feeling down. If you think about that and think about this boy, just a little bit, then I'm sure you'll come up with something perfect. When you're feeling blue, do you want someone to yell at you about it?"

"No. I want them to sit next to me and talk to me. Then I want to eat sweets with them and play games."

"If that's what you think, then that's what you should do."

I tried to nod, but there was one thing that still weighed on my mind. "But what if he really does hate me?"

Skank-san stroked my hair.

"I don't think he does, but on the off chance that is true, I'll be here to comfort you. And then we'll think again about what to do."

"…"

"You'll be fine, little miss. You're brave, aren't you?" she said, patting me on the back. That single blow felt very much like someone kicking a motorcycle engine to make it start. I could feel the power from her palm igniting the engine of my body.

"That's true. I'll try it then. I said so anyway."

"Said what?"

"I told Kiriyuu-kun, if you don't start moving, nothing can begin. So I'll do it. Say, Skank-san, I—"

It was not a hand clapped over my mouth, nor the taste of being made to drink something bitter, that suddenly robbed me of my speech.

"Skank-san?"

It was because I saw her face, which had utterly shifted from her usual smile. In that moment, though we were still inside, I swore I could feel a cold wind blowing through.

Her expression was one of shock, far sharper now than before. It was as if she had completely forgotten there was someone she happened to share a catchphrase with. Like she had seen an alien and a sorcerer and a creature from the center of the earth all at once. As if she had been struck by lightning. That was the sort of face she was making. I had seen this face somewhere before.

"What's wrong?" I asked.

She stared at me as though I had just transformed into a monster.

"Kiriyuu...kun...?"

The word seemed to be dragged out from deep inside her.

"Yeah, that's him. Kiriyuu-kun, the one who draws."

As she took it in, I wondered if my words had somehow grown into a great bouquet of flowers. Her face looked just like ladies on TV, when someone proposed to them.

"What is it?" I asked again, but she did not answer my question.

"Are you...Nanoka?"

"Yes," I said with a nod. Of course I was.

Suddenly, her eyes welled with tears and her face seemed unable to bear the shock. Adults never cry just to surprise children. And yet, I was surprised. I hadn't the faintest clue of why she would be crying.

"I see..."

Nor could I grasp the meaning of her words, as though she had just come to terms with something. And so I could not understand what she did next. She did not squeeze my hands, or stroke my hair. Instead, she wrapped her arms around me tightly, a single tear falling from her eyes.

I was happy to be embraced by someone I loved, but I was taken aback. I had felt the same manner of shock once before, just recently, up on that rooftop.

Skank-san started to cry like a child.

"What's wrong? Hey, Skank-san, what's wrong?"

Although I asked, she did not answer. She merely whispered into my ear, again and again, "So that's what's going on," "How, how?" "I can't believe it," and other things like that. And then, she said, "I'm sorry, I'm sorry, I'm so sorry."

What on earth was she apologizing for?

The kind, brilliant, wonderful Skank-san, who taught me so many things, who gave me hints, and dessert, and always brought me joy... I could not think of a single thing she needed to apologize for.

And yet, she kept on crying, kept on apologizing. Little by little, she gave me the reasons for this apology. And yet, I still did not understand.

"I'm sorry, I'm sorry for saying I wasn't happy," she said, but I was speechless. "I'm sorry for becoming this way. I'm sorry for letting people call me those names."

And finally, she said, "I'm so sorry...Nanoka."

She squeezed me tightly as she said my name. Even as I let out a grunt from the mild discomfort of her embrace, she did not let me go. Just then, I realized something curious, and remembered something even more unusual.

I remembered it because I was so sharp. Twice now she had said my name. Minami-san had said it on that last day, too. And yet I realized that, for some reason, I had forgotten to ever tell either one of them my name.

So then, how was it that they both knew it, and why had I never told her before now? These two mysteries cycloned through my brain.

Perhaps I could ask Skank-san about this mystery. She was clever, after all. As she wept, I spoke all of these mysteries into her ear. She pulled away from me and sat up straight. Her face was messy with snot and tears. *Everyone looks the same when they're crying, huh?*

"There's nothing mysterious about it. I finally understand now. I know why you came here that day. I know why I met you."

No, this absolutely *was* mysterious. She grinned through the tears as I tilted my head, and held up the index finger of her right hand.

"Listen up, little miss. Life is like a pudding."

"Because there's people who like the bitter parts, too?"

"No."

Her hair waved side-to-side.

"There are some bitter parts to life, but there's plenty of sweet happiness stuffed into that same cup. People live for the sake of that sweetness. Thank you, little miss. I've just remembered something, all thanks to you."

"What's that?"

"That I've always loved sweets more than bitter coffee and beer. I won't forget that again."

She squeezed me once more. I thought it curious that she kept doing this, but I seemed to have lost all interest in unraveling these mysteries. As far as I was concerned, the feeling of being in her arms was one of the sweet parts of life.

Finally she stopped crying, but offered no explanation when I asked her what was going on. She said only, "I'm sure you'll be able to understand someday."

Instead, what she offered me was peculiar indeed: the dessert that she had bought for us.

"It suits you perfectly."

There was no dark portion to the pudding she offered me. Everything packed into the cup was a sweet, creamy golden color. My mouth filled with the taste of happiness as I ate it.

As we ate our puddings together, we played our usual game of Othello. The wins and the losses were the same as ever. Someday, I would show her I was stronger.

Before I went home, she gave me courage for tomorrow. She squeezed my hand, and then my whole body, and told me, "You'll be fine, I just know it." With that, I could believe that I truly would.

"Ah," Skank-san said as I donned my shoes and made to step out of the door, as though she had just remembered something.

"What is it?" I asked.

"Oh no, it's just... I was wondering if Granny is happy right now."

I recalled the conversation I'd had with Granny previously. "Yes, she said that she was happy," I replied.

A smile of true happiness spread across Skank-san's face. "I'm glad," she said. Then, she waved her hand as always. "See you later, little miss."

"Yeah, see you next time!"

When I closed the door, I noticed a little black shadow at my feet.

"I didn't forget about you. Sometimes even children have things to take care of."

"Meow."

"I know. I'll give you milk back at my house. Don't tell my mother, though."

She had probably come because she was worried about me. She might be a wicked girl, but I'd seen an American film once that said all bad girls are secretly good deep down. I didn't really understand what it meant to be bad and good at the same time, but I'm sure that they were describing girls just like Miss Bobtail.

We I left the cream-colored building and walked to the embankment where we had first met, long ago.

Life is chock full of happiness.

I repeated those words to myself again and again.

I had that
same
Dream
again

Chapter 9

IT WAS A BRIGHT AND SUNNY DAY as I left my house like always, but unlike always, I did not head to school. I was a good girl and I could not tell a lie. So, that morning, when I told my mother I was leaving, I did not tell her *where* I was headed. Now that's what I call clever.

I did not head to school because I had something far more important to do. *Although in truth, there is probably no reason for me to ever go back to school again,* I thought. As for my studies, I could just have Skank-san tutor me. Even if I didn't have lunch, I would have Granny's sweets to tide me over. I would write letters to Hitomi-sensei now and then. People might say that I *had* to go to school, that elementary school education was compulsory, but what did they do when it *wasn't* necessary?

Now that I thought about it, I'd learned about skipping grades from a movie. I was smart enough that I could probably just do that. Well, no... Like Skank-san had told me, getting smarter wasn't everything. Given that I had only been attending school for that purpose, there was probably no reason for me to go ever again.

As I thought all those things, I arrived at my destination before I knew it.

I hadn't the slightest bit of doubt about coming here today. My arrival was different from the previous time. For one, I did not have my little friend at my side. Plus, it was still morning. The most important change, however, was that I no longer held any notions about attacking *him*.

Like the last time, I rang the doorbell again and again. Like before, it was a sullen woman's voice that I heard through the speaker. Last time, I had replied to that voice with a cheerful greeting. Today however, there was something that I needed to do.

I put all my heart into my words, to be sure to convey how I truly felt.

"It's Koyanagi Nanoka, Kiriyuu-kun's classmate. I'm sorry about what happened last time."

Although the woman could not see me, I bowed my head. You have to be sure to put your whole heart into it when you're apologizing or giving thanks. It's the same whether you're clever or not.

My feelings must have made it through to her because, just like last time, she very kindly said, "Just a moment."

I bowed my head once more when she finally opened the door.

"Good morning. I'm sorry about last time," I repeated. These were my true feelings, as true as when I had called Kiriyuu-kun a coward.

"Good morning. And no, there's nothing for you to apologize for," she said, shaking her head. But that was not true. There was plenty for me to apologize for.

"I'm sorry for leaving without saying a proper goodbye last time, and for saying such terrible things to Kiriyuu-kun."

"It's all right. Hikari is the one who should be apologizing. You came all the way to see him, but he wouldn't even come out of his room. The notes that you brought were beautifully written. I made sure to give them to him. And you dropped in here before going to school today."

Apparently, she really had forgiven me for all the rude things I had done the last time. Still, I thought what she was saying was a little bit wrong, so I told her the reason I had come today.

"I came to talk to Kiriyuu-kun about something. It's not about being his ally, or fighting, or coming to school. It's something more important."

"Something important?"

Kiriyuu's mother was a very kind person. Her face looked like a castle guard in a story. Naturally, it was me that she was guarding against. Not only had I been rude, but I had harmed her son last time I came. However, if I let all that deter me, I would not have come here today. I absolutely had to talk to Kiriyuu-kun.

If I wished to be forgiven, there was only one thing to do. I had to earnestly pour my whole heart out without a single lie:

why I had come here, what I wanted to say, why I felt that way, and who I hoped to become. As people walked their dogs and other children passed by the house on their way to my school, I told Kiriyuu's mother everything.

I believe that you should share what you feel at the bottom of your heart with the person you are talking to. That's probably why I ended up telling Kiriyuu-kun just how cowardly I thought he was.

I had my doubts, but I still wanted to try and explain these things properly to his mother. Just as before, she let me inside the house.

I did not understand why, unlike last time, her eyes appeared to be glistening slightly. As sharp as I was, I could never understand the reason for an adult's tears, no matter how much I thought about it. Even when I asked them, they usually wouldn't tell me. Not Kiriyuu-kun's mother, nor Skank-san, nor Minami-san.

Once inside, she brought me orange juice, just like before. I took only a single sip before heading to the second floor. This time, I did not have Kiriyuu's mother accompany me up. I simply did not feel there was any need. Even she agreed it was probably better that way.

I was cool as a cucumber as I climbed the stairs, despite the nerves I had felt last time. Today, I felt just as I did when climbing the stairs to Skank-san's apartment. Step by step, as though walking towards something, although I don't know if that was happiness or something else.

Skank-san had said that happiness meant being able to think seriously about someone. I wasn't sharp when it came to people.

That much I knew. Thus, I could not come to like others, or think much about them. And so I had decided to think only about myself. And I was sure that I was happy as I traveled here today, having come to this decision.

I began to sing.

"Happiness won't cooome, wandering my way, sooo thaaat's why I set ooout to find it todaaay!"

There was no one to sing along with me. Miss Bobtail was not present, nor was Skank-san, or Minami-san, or Granny. I was having fun singing by myself, but singing is always much more fun when you have someone to accompany you.

I would have to find someone to sing with me.

I stopped before one of the doors and knocked sharply. I'm sure that Kiriyuu must have known that it was not his mother who had knocked.

"Salutations, Kiriyuu-kun," I said. "First off, I have something to say. I'm sorry about last time."

I bowed before the door. Obviously he could not see me, nor did he reply. But I believed that he could hear me. I took a breath.

"I really did want to apologize to you, cross my heart, but that's not why I came here today. There's something waaay more important I need to talk to you about."

I dropped my backpack onto the floor and sat down with my back to the wall. Then, I took one of my notebooks out from my bag. I had a different notebook for every subject: math went in the math notebook, science in the science notebook, and so forth. The one I had brought today was my language arts notebook.

"Now, Kiriyuu-kun, let's start the discussion."

I opened the notebook to the page for class discussions.

"The topic is: what is happiness?"

It was for this purpose, for this conversation, that I had come to Kiriyuu's house today. I did not wish to talk about allies and enemies, or going to school, or whether or not he lacked courage. Only this. If you had asked me why, I'm sure that I would have said it was because having friends and allies meant finding happiness together.

I had thought hard about it the night before, about what it meant to be an ally. I was happy being with Skank-san, who had become happy just thinking about me. I had found happiness in reading Minami-san's stories, who had promised me that she would try to become happy, too. I was happy when I was eating sweets and talking about books with Granny, who had said that being with me made her happy. And so, I wanted to find happiness with Kiriyuu-kun as well. That was what it meant to be an ally. I was sure of it.

Kiriyuu-kun was my partner in class discussions. And a discussion like this necessitated a notebook more than it did the contents of a fridge.

"Let's start with a review. I'll read out everything that we've thought of so far. In the very first discussion, we discussed when we feel happy: eating cookies with ice cream on top, eating Granny's ohagi, eating sweets your mom baked, reading books, singing songs with friends, having Hamburg steak for dinner, when your mom and dad get home early, traveling with your family, eating your favorite ice cream."

I purposefully avoided reading just one of the items.

"During the next discussion, we talked about times when we didn't feel happy: seeing cockroaches, when there's natto in the school lunch... You added when there's seaweed salad in the lunches, but I didn't agree with that. I think seaweed is delicious."

There was still no sound from Kiriyuu-kun's room.

"After we listed a lot of things that *weren't* happiness, we talked about something a little different: whether *not* being happy was the opposite of happiness, and whether we are happy when the *opposite* of something we dislike happens. But we came to the conclusion that wasn't true. We wouldn't be happy just because we *didn't* have natto in our lunches. You added that you wouldn't be happy just because there wasn't seaweed salad, either. At least, not if there wasn't kara-age in its place."

Kiriyuu-kun still said nothing.

"We had a number of discussions after that, and then it was class observation day. When we presented, I said that having my mother and father there made me happy. What I said wasn't a lie, but I didn't get to explain that it's not all there is to happiness. What you presented wasn't what you were really thinking either, was it?"

No reply.

"When we had our review session afterwards, I asked you why you thought that about happiness, but you couldn't answer. But I didn't come here to talk about the fact that you lied, so let's keep going."

Nothing still.

"Starting here are the discussions that we had while you weren't at school. The discussions continued with Hitomi-sensei taking your place. It wasn't much different from how we did it when you were here, but this time I thought about *why* I feel happy when I do."

"Why?"

Kiriyuu-kun interrupted me at last, without any preamble. It was so soft that I probably would not have heard it if my hearing had not been as good as it was.

I was not surprised to hear him. Kiriyuu-kun was kind, and I knew that he could never do something as horrible as ignore a classmate.

"Why what? Why was I partners with Hitomi-sensei? That's because our class is an even number. It's good that no one else besides you was away."

"No..."

There was silence this time before he spoke again. It was probably because he had taken a number of deep breaths. Deep breathing was necessary, after all, for opening up your heart.

I waited for a long while. I would wait for as long as I had to. I felt as though I could hear his soft breathing from the other side of the door. I'll say it once more: Kiriyuu-kun was kind. So, if I waited, he would respond. I was certain of it.

"I'm not...talking about...Hitomi-sensei...I'm talking about... you."

See?

"Me?"

Even with the door between us, Kiriyuu-kun could probably see how I tilted my head. Even if other people couldn't see it, I'm sure that he could. That's the impression I got, anyway.

"Why...?" he asked again.

"Mm?"

"Why...did you come back?"

Aha. I patted my fist onto my palm in realization. "You mean," I asked. "Why did I come back, after you told me not to?"

"Yeah..."

"If you don't want me to be here, I'll leave right now."

There was no reply. Instead, he asked me the same question.

"Why?"

"Okay?"

"How come?"

"Mm-hm?"

"Why do you care so much about me?"

His voice sounded different this time. Previously, he had wanted a reason. Now he sounded as though he truly did not understand.

I'm sure that the two "why"s carried incredibly different meanings for Kiriyuu-kun. However, that had nothing to do with me. I already had answers to both of those questions.

"Well, that's easy. Because I decided to come, and because I decided to care."

"No, that's, uh..."

"And because I like your drawings."

I sensed his breath stop on the other side of the door. I held no illusions that he had suddenly died or something, so I continued.

"People who can make things that I can't are amazing. The sweets that Granny makes, the stories Minami-san writes, the pictures you draw. I can't make any of those, so I think it's amazing. That's why I'm always saying how amazing you are."

I wouldn't try to force him to show them off anymore. Forcing him to do so when he didn't want to wouldn't make him happy.

"Minami-san is a friend of mine, though I haven't seen her in a while."

"You...have a friend?"

I was a little peeved at that. I was not angry, but people at least needed to be made aware when they had said something rude.

"Seriously? Even *I* have friends. I have very wonderful friends."

"Oh, I see."

Yes, that's right, I indicated with a nod.

"Ah!"

Just then, a shout came from Kiriyuu-kun's room. Had he spotted a bug or something? *Serves him right for making fun of me,* I thought with a smug little grin, when suddenly he called to me from within, sounding much more harried than normal. I prepared myself to be annoyed when he asked me to come in and deal with the bug for him, but instead, he said, "K-Koyanagi-san, shouldn't you be getting to school?"

"Ah...that time already, is it?"

I did not have a wristwatch or a cell phone, so I had no way of telling how much time had passed.

"Won't you...be late?"

"Doesn't matter. I don't need to go to school."

He seemed surprised at this. Rightfully so, to hear someone as diligent and clever as me say such a thing.

"I-I think you should go..."

"But you aren't going, are you? It's fine. I have something more important to take care of, anyway. Kids in our class have gotten time off for their relatives' weddings and stuff anyway."

"Something...more important...?"

"Finding happiness with you."

As far as I was concerned, this was far more important than going to school. I wanted to be his ally. At first I thought that this was only because Hitomi-sensei had told me to do so, but as I thought about it, I realized something. I had always felt that way, deep down. Nothing had changed. I wanted to be allies with the kind and gentle Kiriyuu-kun, who was the only one to talk to me when I was feeling down. Who was the only person who spoke to me when no one came to my observation day. That was all. The sweet Kiriyuu-kun who never ignored me, even when he said he hated me. Yes, that was all.

All that had changed was how I hoped to do it. Previously, I made that feeling known by fighting on his behalf, now I would find out how to become happy alongside him. That way sounded like a lot more fun, so I decided to continue our discussion of happiness, even putting aside all we had talked about in school.

"So, I'm gonna ask again: What does happiness mean to you, Kiriyuu-kun?"

"K-Koyanagi-san..."

He seemed troubled, probably because I was no longer referring to him as "spineless," just as I would be shocked if Kiriyuu-kun suddenly picked a fight. Or as shocked as I was when Ogiwara-kun ignored me.

"I want to hear how you feel about it now."

"Koyanagi-san...you really should get to school."

"I told you, it's fine. So, what's your happiness?"

"You can't be skipping school..."

"Weird to think that's bad for me, but it's okay for you. So, it must be fine. Here, I'll say it myself: This wasn't my idea, but according to a very special friend, this is what happiness is about."

"You need to go to school."

"I'm already smart! I told you, I'm not going!" I said, shouting without thinking. Although I was a little embarrassed, I could not take back what I had said. I quickly offered a quiet "I'm sorry."

That was when I realized something and came to a decision. If you wanted to be someone's friend, you couldn't hide any shocking secrets from them. So, I decided to reveal just how I was feeling.

"I'm sorry. I didn't wanna say it, but our classmates have been ignoring me."

"Huh...?"

"I'm sure you know I didn't have any friends in our class to begin with, but at least there were some people I could talk to, and if I greeted them, everyone replied. But now, everyone's ignoring me."

Talking about painful things hurts as much as experiencing them, but it also has the mysterious power to open up your heart, in the same way as deep breathing.

"I don't want to go to a place full of children like that," I said. "More importantly, I think it's a lot more fun solving difficult questions with you."

As I was speaking, I realized something incredibly important.

"Y'know something?" I asked. "I'm gonna come here from now on. So, you should teach me how to draw. I'll never learn how to draw as well as you, no matter how long I go to school."

I finally realized it.

"Hm, wonder what I should teach you in return. Life is like the seat next to you, y'know?"

It wasn't him who needed allies. It was me.

"If someone's forgotten their textbook, then you have to share it. And, well, if you have to see someone's face every day, it'd better be someone you don't hate."

"I..."

"Yes? What?"

When he finally spoke, his voice was somehow even quieter than usual.

"I want you to teach me...how to...be like you."

His voice was as soft as a flower's whisper, but I heard it. And then, I was disappointed, wondering why he would care about such a thing.

"You don't want to be like me. If you were like me, then you wouldn't be able to draw those wonderful pictures. My mother saw a lion I'd drawn and she thought it was the Tower of the Sun. I hated it."

He was silent again.

"So if a magician ever offers to turn you into someone else, the person you should change into is you. Got it?"

He didn't say a single word about that. Instead, after a long, empty pause, he said something else.

"You really should go to school."

I was shocked. I hadn't expected him to say that again. I had made my conviction clear, again and again. I had made up my mind, but he didn't know that, of course. Obviously, this bothered me.

"Why? Normally you never oppose the things I say in class, but you're nothing but rude today. I guess you hate me so much you'd rather see me go somewhere where everyone ignores me?"

I said it as a joke, imagining him shaking his head so vigorously I'd be able to tell it even on the other side of the door. But when a reply from him did not come, I began to feel uneasy.

The words he had said the last time drifted out from my heart bit by bit, as if wanting air. If I were to let them all out at once, that dark, terrible thing would take root again inside my heart, and all my courage would be trapped like a butterfly caught in a spider's web.

Before I could let that happen, I had to be sure that Kiriyuu-kun didn't actually hate me. If he did, he would never talk to me this much. Indeed, those words had probably just leapt out of his mouth all on their own. *And so, I will ask him the same question once more, and wait for his reply,* I thought, before he put a stop to that.

Life is the same as a beautifully painted dessert. Sometimes you just can't understand how it got that way. Kiriyuu-kun still said nothing. But his feelings and actions silenced me, and I felt that monster inside of me sinking back down to the bottom of the sea.

I heard the door unlock. Then I saw the doorknob turning, slowly but surely.

Perhaps because the window was open inside the room, a strong wind blew in my face, sending my bangs dancing and forcing me to shut my eyes. When I opened them again, I saw Kiriyuu-kun standing before me, countless sheets of paper dancing behind him, carried by the wind. *Has his hair grown a bit longer?* As I wondered this, looking at his face, one of the papers came flying towards me, plastering itself against my own.

Unable to breathe, I quickly snatched it away. When I looked at it, the smile that spread across my cheeks must have rivaled even Skank-san's.

Kiriyuu-kun was the complete opposite, crouching in the doorway, a tragic look upon his face. There might have even been a bit of dampness to his eyes.

"What's wrong?" I asked.

"I'm... I'm sorry," he said.

A lot of people seemed to be apologizing to me lately. And yet, I had not received a single apology from the people I actually wanted to hear it from.

"Why are you apologizing?"

Hadn't he said that he hated me? If that was true, then I couldn't say that it didn't bother me, but then I had been the one to call him a coward. Fair is fair.

Kiriyuu-kun looked me straight in the eye.

"Y-you..."

"I what?"

"You're getting ignored...because of me."

"That's not true." I shook my head. "It isn't your fault. It's because all those idiots in our class are too stupid to even know right from wrong."

"But it *is* true."

Even as he looked straight at me, the tears flowed from Kiriyuu-kun's eyes. This had been happening a lot lately, too.

"What is?" I asked.

"That my father...stole something..."

I was quiet. Indeed, I had already known this was true. Even so, I shook my head. I tried to imagine just how tragic a thing this must be for Kiriyuu-kun. I don't know whether my imaginings truly reached the depth of it, though I stretched them as far as I could. If they did not, I had no idea how much further I would have to reach to get there. Even so, I proudly shook my head.

"Even if he did, so what?" I looked into his eyes to guide him. He was wrong, after all. "Even if your father stole, it doesn't change the fact that he always greeted me kindly. More than the kids in our class, who I see every day. Moreover, that's no reason for people to ignore me, or for me not to go to school. And it's no reason for them to talk badly about you. But this conversation isn't about your father, anyway."

Indeed, out of all the bad things that had happened, not once had Kiriyuu-kun ever done anything wrong.

"The ones who are wrong are the people who don't know that. The fact that I'm not going to school is those people's fault, too."

So, there was no reason for Kiriyuu-kun to be sad, or to cry. That was what I meant, but life is like when you get off of a teacup ride, and sometimes you end up walking in the opposite direction from the way you mean to.

Not only did Kiriyuu-kun not stop crying, the tears began to drip from his face. Although, I was not sure which of my words made him so sad. Since I did not know, I was unsure of what to do to make him feel better. So, I shuffled closer and put my hand atop his on the floor. When Skank-san did that for me, I could feel my heart quieting.

He looked surprised, but just as I had done that that day at Skank-san's, he squeezed my hand back.

I intended to sit there, quietly holding his hand until the tears stopped, but I could not do so. Kiriyuu-kun was still crying, but he said something I never imagined he would.

"Do you...want...to go to school...together?"

"Huh?" I said, flabbergasted at this sudden proposal.

In the moments it took me to pull myself together, I noticed how he flinched back at this, and I realized something.

"Did you just say 'together'?"

"Yeah..."

My hand ached from how tightly he was gripping it, but in my surprise, I completely forgot that pain.

"Wh...why?"

His lips quavered at my heartfelt question. He was probably searching for the perfect words. I understood that feeling, so I was happy to wait as long as he needed me to.

"I...told a lie," he finally said. "I...lied. I'm still afraid...that I might get made fun of again. And I lied...to Hitomi-sensei. So...I want to apologize to her, and tell her the truth."

The tears still had not stopped. And yet I had never seen such strength in his eyes. I had no idea that he could show such courage. I was desperate to know the reason.

"What do you mean, 'the truth'?"

"About...what happiness is."

Just then, a scene flashed before my eyes. Clearly, in voice and vision. It was not of Kiriyuu-kun speaking, but of me, saying something low enough that only Kiriyuu-kun could hear. A single word I spoke on observation day: *coward*.

So he *had* been lying. Even knowing this, I felt no sadness or irritation.

"I don't care about the other people, but I want to tell the truth to Hitomi-sensei, and to you."

I was thrilled.

"I...actually think there's something I need to apologize to Hitomi-sensei for, too," I said.

"Huh?"

"She was really sad that she never got to see you when she came by. I forgot to tell you, but she told me to say that she would be waiting for you, as long as it took."

I left in such a hurry the last time that I forgot. As I told him this, the tears began to drip down his face once more. Still, even his tears were no match for the sparkling in his eyes.

"I want to see her."

I felt the same.

"But are you sure?" I asked. "If you go to school, those idiots who were making fun of you will be there."

And who were ignoring me.

Up until now, I felt that Kiriyuu-kun should fight those boys, but thanks to Skank-san, I now knew that was not his way of fighting. Now I had seen this with my own eyes.

His shoulders trembled at my words, just a little. But he looked me straight in the eyes and, with his own strength, shook himself free of the devil clinging to his back.

"I really...don't want to...but...I think I'll...be fine."

This time, I did not know what to say.

"Even if they make fun of me," he said. "Even if they call me names, I think I'll be fine, as long as you're my ally."

I couldn't have said why, but tears of relief welled in my eyes, despite the fact that people only cry when they're sad. And yet I wept with relief, knowing that when Kiriyuu said that he hated me, it was a lie.

But the tears did not fall. It was weird to cry if you weren't sad, after all. Instead, I looked into his eyes and nodded firmly.

"Of course. I've never once been your enemy."

More tears streamed from him. It was curious. It felt strange that he should be crying.

He squeezed my hand again. "I really think that you should go to school, too," he said.

"And why is that?"

Finally, I was able to hear the reason.

"You're not like me. You're good at studying, and smart, and strong, and I just know you're gonna be someone important someday...that's why you can't skip school."

I was glad for this praise, but he said something else that made me even happier.

"So, let's go to school together...I'm your ally, too."

No matter how much time passed, I would never be able to find the right words to describe how I felt in that moment. Even at Minami-san's age, or Skank-san's age, or even Granny's, never ever would I be able to label the smell or the taste of what was spreading through my heart.

I was painted with such wonderful colors that not a drop of black might be found within, but nor could it be called white. It was a color that I'm not even sure existed in the world. Perhaps a brand-new color had been born in that very moment.

I could not explain what it was, so I can only offer my usual phrase instead: Life is like...my ally.

"As long as I have you, Hikari, that's enough."

"Huh...?"

"You made a good point, Kiriyuu-kun, so I may as well go to school. You'll be there as my ally, won't you?"

He cried again, just a little. He smiled too, the tears still lingering in his eyes. It was the first time I had seen his smile in ages.

Seeing an ally's smile is always a joyous thing. And so I smiled too, with my own joy.

"Well, if that's your decision, then hurry up and get ready! We're already super late!"

"O-on it!"

He stood quickly, roughly rubbing the tears away with his sleeve and shutting the door. He had still been in his pajamas, so he was probably changing.

I stood outside and prepared myself to leave as soon as he was ready. At first, I thought that I would just wait there quietly, but then I thought that I had better tell his mother we were going. She might be able to call the school so that we wouldn't be marked tardy.

I told Kiriyuu-kun my plans through the door and walked down the hall, headed for the stairs. Just as I rounded the corner, I let out a wholly unattractive scream.

"Aah!"

Stunned, I fell down onto my behind. In front of me was Kiriyuu-kun's mother. She was crouching in front of the stairs as if trying to hide, with tears in her eyes.

Everyone seems to be crying lately. Is it some new trend? Or is it contagious, like a yawn? I wondered. As I sat there still on the floor, Kiriyuu's mother gripped my hand, the same one that Kiriyuu-kun had gripped just minutes ago.

"Thank you," she said.

It's probably the first time she has seen him come out of his room in ages, I thought.

"Of course," I replied earnestly.

But then, she said something strange. "I should have told him that, too."

What could that possibly mean? As I pondered this, I heard Kiriyuu-kun's door open. I looked back, and there he was in the clothes he often wore, a backpack on his back. *All ready to go,* I thought. By the time I stood, Kiriyuu's mother was already descending the stairs.

I was not as hasty as her, so I waited for Kiriyuu-kun. I realized I was still holding my notebook, and went to put it away in my bag.

And then...

"That's..."

There was something in my hand that was not my notebook. Kiriyuu-kun, coming up behind me, noticed it as well. I let him know what I was truly feeling.

"Can I...have this?" I asked.

I might be refused, I thought. No, he would definitely refuse, if he was his usual self. But he didn't refuse. He nodded, a slight look of embarrassment on his face.

I was glad, but I did not understand why. Still, I decided I would hang it up in my room at home.

"Should we get going?" I asked.

"Yeah," he replied.

The light in his eyes shone brightly.

As we arrived at school, Kiriyuu's fingers gripped onto my jacket. I was sure that he had no intention of touching a girl's behind, so I said nothing. Besides, I knew exactly how he was feeling. Because I understood this, I puffed out my chest. It did not have the volume of Skank-san's or Hitomi-sensei's, but I puffed it out with all my might nonetheless. If you cowered in fear, your enemies would think they had won. So at times like these, it was better to thrust out your chest and pretend to be strong, even if it was a lie. My father taught me that once, as we walked along a road at night.

I led Kiriyuu-kun in through the back door of the classroom, and it was as though time had stopped. Everyone stared at us, not moving a muscle. But time soon rebooted itself, and everyone averted their eyes, muttering. After that, only one person was looking at us. That person was, naturally...

"All right, quiet down everyone. This is still class time. You two are here just in time. You're a little bit late, but class is just getting started, so don't worry."

I grabbed my skirt and bent my knees in greeting to Hitomi-sensei, curtsying like a princess. I was sure that I heard her reply "*Merci*," even if she did not say it aloud.

Kiriyuu-kun nervously bowed his head to Hitomi-sensei, then took his seat. *Oh, right,* I thought. "Sensei, I forgot all of my textbooks, so I'm going to share with Kiriyuu-kun," I announced.

A murmuring kicked up in the classroom again, but Hitomi-sensei only said, "Make sure you bring them tomorrow," and allowed me to move my desk closer to Kiriyuu's. I actually hadn't brought the right books, since I had never intended to come to school today. The two of us placed our backpacks on the shelf in the back and soon we were ready to start.

We were about fifteen minutes into first period, language arts. *Perfect, right?* I thought, sending Kiriyuu-kun a wink, but he did not notice and it dissipated into the air.

As usual, today's lesson was about happiness. We split into pairs to discuss a short story we had read in the previous class, in preparation for our final presentation.

I did not think that Kiriyuu-kun had read the story, so first I would have to explain it to him. Or so I thought. In fact, he had already read it. He had diligently read *all* of the handouts Hitomi-sensei brought for him while he was locked away in his room.

We discussed the story, and Kiriyuu-kun was even more reserved than usual. We talked about whether suddenly having enough of something you once lacked was happiness, or whether being satisfied with not having enough was happiness, and so forth. Since Kiriyuu-kun still had his head down, I did most of the talking. As we talked, I was fully aware of the glances our classmates stole in our direction here and there. They all must have been weird in the head to be so interested when they were ignoring us.

Somewhere in the middle, Hitomi-sensei came over to us. She always made the rounds during discussion. As she approached, we gave the morning greetings that we had not previously been able to.

"Good morning, Hitomi-sensei," I said.

"Morning. And good morning to you too, Kiriyuu-kun."

"Good morning," Kiriyuu replied in a teeny tiny voice, his head still bowed.

But he was by no means afraid—he had wanted to see Hitomi-sensei, after all. There was a different word for this sort of feeling: unease.

Even I had times when I was uneasy. When I had that fight with my mother before class observation day was just one such time. So I knew that when you're in an uneasy circumstance, you have to do something about it yourself, sooner or later.

I gripped Kiriyuu's hand, just out of sight of Hitomi-sensei, hoping to share my courage with him. However, there was no need. He returned the squeeze once, then pulled away. Before Hitomi-sensei could ask anything, he lifted his head.

"S-sensei, I found a d-different answer about...what happiness is. Different from what I s-said on observation day."

Although his words were faltering and his voice soft, he was presenting. I cheered him on silently. My thoughts were only on him. That was the happiness Skank-san had found.

So, what was Kiriyuu-kun's happiness? Both he and I knew the answer the entire time. I was proud of him, thrilled at the prospect of hearing it out of his own mouth for the first time. I was surely still his only fan in the class, so it made sense, didn't it?

"Oh? What would that be?"

Perhaps Hitomi-sensei was surprised at this sudden presentation, but her face did not betray it. She entreated him politely, her expression warm. It was the sort of face that suggested she would listen to whatever it was he had to say.

Kiriyuu-kun looked her straight in the eye, his lips hanging limply. Suddenly I realized that everyone else in class was looking our way. I thought this surprising, given how little they had minded him before this, but it also felt right. The chance for everyone to hear how Kiriyuu-kun truly felt.

Now he just had to say it.

"M-my happiness is...draw—"

He stopped mid-sentence. Hitomi-sensei waited for him patiently, her face kind, but I stared at him wide-eyed. *How can he have gotten this far, only to get afraid again?* I thought, and maybe I gave him a critical look. Maybe I had misjudged him. It was true that I was his ally, but honestly I started to think that he was still a bit of a weakling. For that I must apologize. I remembered Granny's words: *That boy might be less cowardly than you think.*

Kiriyuu-kun breathed in and out several times and bit his lip, then puffed out his chest and said "My happiness is..."

"Yes?"

"When my friend says that they like my drawings, and when they are sitting beside me."

Honestly, life really is like a game of Othello. Because even when there are dark, unpleasant things, there's a bright and lovely side, too? No, that isn't it.

It's because a single shining piece can turn one's dark feelings right around.

It should come as no surprise that I wanted to tell my special friend about this wonderful day. So, after school ended, I said a rushed farewell to Kiriyuu-kun, ran home and collected Miss Bobtail, and headed right back out toward that cream-colored building.

"Happiness won't cooome! Wandering my way, sooo!"

"Meow?" My black-furred friend made a strange face at my abnormally enthusiastic delivery.

"What?"

"Meow."

"Look, it's fine to sing like this sometimes. I mean, honestly you could even do it all the time, but sometimes you have an extra good day. I bet even you have days like this sometimes?"

"Meow," she replied, uninterested. Perhaps this was not such a good day for her. I attempted to share my good mood.

"Thaaat's why I set ooout to find it todaaay!"

"Meow meow meow."

Although she looked exasperated, eventually she began to sing along. *What was with the act?* I thought. She was trying to be so grown up. But perhaps the boys were taken with those insincere parts of her. *If there is anything I can learn from her, it is the way to a boy's heart,* I thought as we walked along the embankment.

The sky was blue, the grass was green, and the dirt was brown. The soft earth of the path was auburn, cut for easy strolling. The wind was clear, and every person was their own color. Everything was painted with varying hues, and I loved every one of them. But it was when I spied the cream-colored building that my heart leapt the highest.

I laid out all the things that I wished to talk to Skank-san about.

First, I absolutely had to thank her. It was only because of her advice that I was able to find such joy inside my heart. Then I would tell her about every single thing that happened today. I'd talk simply about the unimportant parts, and at more length about the more important stuff. Of course, I would have to stress the unimportant parts that were connected to the important parts, so as to embellish the message. She would probably be surprised to hear me say that Kiriyuu-kun was not the sort of boy who ever did the things he did today.

Still, I thought that I should be emphatic about the fact that Kiriyuu-kun really might have some courage, and that Granny was the only one able to see it.

I was bubbling with excitement. More excitement than I felt upon watching cocoa powder dissolve into warm milk and the smell of chocolate wafting through the air.

The cream-colored, cake-like building was suited perfectly to cocoa. My excitement reached a fever pitch as I reached the staircase, but as I set foot on the first muddy step, I noticed something unusual: Miss Bobtail did not climb the stairs with me.

"What's wrong?" I asked, but she did not reply. "You don't want any milk?"

She said nothing. I moved to pick her up, thinking that she might be injured somehow, but she slipped out of my arms.

"You're a weirdo. Fine. Wait there, then."

"Meow," she replied finally, her voice very soft.

Well, even cats probably had days that were not so fun, so surely there were days when they had no interest in climbing stairs, either.

Although my thoughts were on my friend's behavior, my heart was still focused on the things I would talk about with Skank-san. I proceeded to her door, and after plotting out most of the conversation, rang the bell.

Ding-dong, I heard from inside. *Hm?* I wondered, looking up. The rather ugly writing on the nameplate beside her door seemed to have vanished. Had she finally rewritten it? I had told her before, my writing was very good. I could have rewritten it for her, if she liked.

I waited, but she did not come out, so I rang the bell one more time. Then I heard a noise from inside. Maybe she was just waking up. What a sleepyhead! I waited for a while, giggling to myself, but still she did not appear.

She must be in, I thought, knocking this time. As I did, I greeted the door with an enthusiastic "Gooood afternoooon!"

A short time after, I heard the door unlock, and the doorknob turned. I always overflowed with anticipation when it was time to see my friend. And yet, when the door opened, that anticipation vanished into smoke.

Something occurred that I had never imagined.

It was not Skank-san who opened the door. It was a man, around the same age as her. I'm sure that the man and I shared the same expression as we looked at each other: surprise. The kind-looking gentleman opened his eyes wide, goggling at me. I'm certain that I was the first to realize who the other must be.

"Are you Skank-san's boyfriend?" I asked.

She was an incredibly lovely woman, so it was not at all

surprising that she might have someone special in her life. If that was the case, then I simply had to introduce myself.

"Pleased to meet you. I'm Koyanagi Nanoka. I'm a friend of Skank-san's," I said politely.

But the young man furrowed his brows, making a face of utter confusion.

"Is she out right now?" I asked.

Despite my very simple question, the man tilted his head. "Um...Nanoka-chan, was it?" he asked.

"Yes, that's right."

"I think you've got the wrong address. This is my place. There's no one here named...*Skank?*"

Any further and his head might swivel all the way around, I thought.

"That's not true. I've never met you before, but I've been here plenty of times. Is Skank-san trying to play a prank on me?"

Maybe she is planning some kind of surprise, I thought, but that didn't seem right. The man gave a troubled laugh.

"You really shouldn't be using words like that. 'Skank,' that is."

"But it's Skank-san's name."

"Mm...well, either way, there's no one here by that name, so I'm sure you're mistaken. Maybe you've got the wrong building? You should double-check."

"I know it's here! I was just here yesterday!"

The sudden loudness of my voice came as surely as the memory of being here. This young man, who knew nothing of the dark unease that swelled in my heart, looked even more troubled.

"I was here yesterday too, and you didn't come by."

"You're lying! You weren't here! I was with Skank-san!"

"Mm, what to do here..." he said, frustrated.

I knew that when an adult expressed their frustration to a child directly, it meant they were thinking about how to shut the child up.

"I've got it," he said. "Maybe you were dreaming, and in that dream, you came to a building that looked like this one? When I was a kid, I spent lots of time searching for the places that I saw in my dreams, but I never found them."

"Dreaming...?"

No, that couldn't be. I knew that Skank-san had been here, that we had played Othello together. Eating pudding, holding her hand—none of that had been a dream. I was certain, from the bottom of my heart, but there was one single memory that drifted through my mind then. That memory's name was Minami-san.

Even by my own cleverness, I could not explain all these mysteries—the mysteries of Skank-san and Minami-san. If I could explain it by my own reckoning, there were only three possible explanations: lies, magic, or dreams.

I figured it must be a lie on this young man's part, but his distress appeared genuine. I didn't get a lying smell from him, at least.

As I stood there in silence, the young man said, "Hold on," and stepped back inside. When he returned, he had a brown Papico in his hand.

"Here, take this. It's hot today. I don't want you to get heat stroke."

The Papico was cool and pleasant, but I knew when I saw it:
this place truly did not belong to Skank-san anymore. Her freezer
never had any Papico in it.

"How could she have moved out overnight...?"

"I mean, no one could. But anyway, I've lived here for four years."

Four years. For a child as young as me, that was an intermi-
nable length of time. I knew. I did not understand it, but I knew
another mystery had occurred.

I thanked him for the treat and left. He saw me off with a
warm, "See you."

I walked along the cream-colored wall and descended the
stairs to find my friend waiting for me. That was when I realized
something. "You knew she wasn't here, didn't you?"

My friend did not reply. Instead, she just began walking
ahead of me. It was the same way we had walked many times before. I followed behind her, sharing her feelings. Minami-san, and
now Skank-san. Mystery after mystery was befalling my friends.
Where had they gone? When I didn't understand something, it
was best to ask someone who had lived far longer than I. After all,
they had probably had the same experiences before.

As we walked along, I tore open the Papico bottle with my
teeth to taste what was inside. I took one mouthful, then another,
considering it.

"This really is kinda bitter."

I was not a fan of the taste of coffee. I waited until the contents of the bottle had melted entirely and offered it to some
passing ants.

Chapter 10

WHEN I ARRIVED at Granny's house, dripping with sweat, there was a note tacked to the wooden door yet again. It had the same message as before. I stepped in through the door, wiped my little friend's feet, took off my shoes, and quietly entered the house. My footsteps sounded different than before because I was wearing sandals today. So instead of the slippery sound of my socks, there was the padding of bare feet upon the floorboards. I had really hoped that Skank-san might compliment those sandals.

I hoped I could show Granny my sandals too, and that she would know where Skank-san had gone, so we could go there at once. Then we would eat ice cream and talk about Kiriyuu-kun.

The house was so quiet that I thought I could hear the faint voice of the trees the house was built from. I walked down the hall, wondering if Granny might be up on the second floor again, but I found her in her bedroom.

Perhaps the sound of my opening the glass door awoke her. She was lying on her side on her bed in that mild, air-conditioned room, smiling gently at me.

"Come in," she said.

"Oh, sorry. Were you napping?"

"It's fine, I was just waking up."

"That's good. Were you having a nice dream?" I asked.

She grinned at me. "Yes, I had that same dream again," she said, sitting up in bed with a more languid motion than usual and opening the curtains. Unlike in the living room, the sun shone dimly in here. The painting hung on the wall seemed to shine with its own light.

"There's some orange juice in the fridge," she said, as I attempted to close the sliding door.

I went to the kitchen and returned with two little juice boxes. She took one from me with a "thank you," and set it down on the bed. The sweet and sour tang of the orange juice washed away the bitter taste that still lingered in my mouth.

"Did it go well?" she asked simply. I nodded.

Normally, this was the part where I would start talking, my words spilling out like a drumroll, but I did nothing of the sort.

"Did something happen?" she asked again. It was obvious to her.

"Yeah. It went well with that boy from my class," I said in a voice that sounded like it was drowning. "But...Skank-san is gone."

I told her everything that had happened that day. Actually, I started with the day before. I told her about my depression regarding Kiriyuu-kun, Skank-san's advice, the fact that she had suddenly started crying, and the wonderful coincidence of us sharing a catchphrase.

Then I told her about today. About how Skank-san had vanished, the strange man now living in her home, the ice cream he gave me that I didn't like, and how this was all far more mysterious than when Minami-san had disappeared.

She listened to my tale and told me that she did not know where Skank-san had gone. To my regret, one more mystery floated through my mind. I decided to ask her about it.

"Skank-san disappeared just like Minami-san. The fact that they're gone makes me feel really lonely, but it doesn't feel like it did when Kiriyuu-kun told me he hated me."

"I see," she said with a nod. That was Granny for you. She knew everything. "It sounds like you aren't despairing, then."

I could not write the kanji for *zetsubou,* "despair."

"Maybe it's because you already know in your heart that you'll meet Skank-san and Minami-san again someday," she said, putting the small, curious relief that I felt into words.

"Exactly," I replied. "I don't have any proof though, like a detective in a mystery story would."

"That's true." She narrowed her eyes and nodded. "Still, I'm sure that you're right. Don't worry. You will definitely see them again someday."

"Yeah, I'm sure of that, too," I said with a firm nod.

"You have the power to see the future, after all," she said.

"I still wanted to talk and play Othello with her some more, though."

"But now you have a friend in your class. Why don't you practice with him?"

"That's true. I don't know if he also has the power to see the future, though."

She tittered at this, as though she was somehow remembering his face. No, that was impossible. She had never met Kiriyuu-kun. She was probably just thinking about her own friend who liked to draw.

"Skank-san asked me if you were happy."

"Did she?"

"I told her that you said that you were happy, but is that because you get to think about your artist friend?"

She tittered again. "Yes, perhaps. Plus, I think about you, and about my family."

"So, would you say that happiness is thinking seriously about someone?"

"Oh my, is your presentation day approaching soon?"

Now that's what they call hitting the nail on the head. However, there was another reason why I asked this question.

"Actually, I just really want to know the answer. Although this assignment *is* complicated."

That was truly how I felt. The assignment was always on my mind.

"There are different kinds of happiness," I said. "A lot of stuff has happened lately. I've asked different people about what happiness is, and the answers they've found. For Minami-san, it was being recognized. For Skank-san, it was thinking about someone else, and for Kiriyuu-kun, it was being with friends. I think each answer is true for them, but I still haven't found a way to describe the happiness inside of me. It's really hard to pick just one thing. Life is like a bento box."

"And how is that?"

"I can't fit in everything I like. And I still don't know how big that bento box is, or what it's called. Granny, if Hitomi-sensei gave you an assignment to say what happiness was, what would your answer be?"

It was a super hard question, but it seemed like she held the answer. She looked up at the sky through the window, as though remembering something from long ago.

"Happiness is..."

"Yes?"

"Being able to say that you're happy right now."

Of all the answers I had received, hers was the easiest to understand, and the one that sunk most easily into my heart. And yet...

"I don't think I could understand that without living a reeeally long time."

"That's true. The happiness I feel is my own, as someone who has lived far longer than you. It's different from your happiness. You have to find your own, Nacchan."

In the end, no matter how much I learned, I would have to think about this myself. As we drank our juice together, gazing at the picture on the wall, I suddenly remembered what I had in my bag.

"Oh, right! I got a picture from Kiriyuu-kun."

I pulled the sheet of paper from my backpack. Knowing Kiriyuu-kun as well as I did, it was impressive that he had shown me a picture at all, but since he had *given* it to me, I couldn't pass up a chance to show it off.

It was a picture of a flower. Looking upon this colored pencil drawing, the creases of Granny's face deepened.

"It's...so lovely."

"Isn't it? I can't believe he was hiding his talent. That's what they call a waste, right? I bet if he keeps practicing, he'll be as amazing at drawing as your friend."

"Heh heh, my friend is amazing, then? If you say so, then perhaps it's true."

"Absolutely," I said, unyielding.

Then I sat down on the end of Granny's bed, and talked about *Our Seven Days' War,* because I had not gotten to talk about it with Ogiwara. When I asked about how stupid the adults were in the book, she laughed and said that there are far more stupid adults than smart ones, and that just because an adult was smart didn't mean that they were a good person.

I loved talking about stories. I wish I could discuss Minami-san's story in the same way, but just as I thought of this, the clock chimed. It was time to go home.

As I stood up, Granny lay back down, going back to her nap. I headed to the door with Miss Bobtail in tow, quietly so as not to disturb Granny. In all honesty, I should have left then, but I stopped.

"Hey, Granny?"

I felt uneasy.

"You won't disappear too, will you?"

She did not reply. Instead, I could hear contented sounds of her breathing. Careful not to disturb her, I fell quiet and left the wooden house with my little friend at my side.

I visited the cream-colored apartment building many times after that day, but Skank-san was never there.

After Skank-san disappeared, I had only two choices of destination after school. One was Granny's house atop the hill. The other was...

"I'm not really good at Othello, though."

"Well then, I'll let you go first."

I had started collecting Miss Bobtail after school and heading to Kiriyuu-kun's house. The first time I had shown up with my Othello set in tow, he was surprised, but his mother happily brought me orange juice. After a few visits, the shock finally wore off, and Kiriyuu-kun and I played Othello and drew pictures happily together. It was good for each of us to have something we were better at.

When I was at Kiriyuu's house, my little friend always waited outside. She was rather shy, after all, and so was Kiriyuu-kun. Once, I invited him to come to Granny's house, but he just froze, looking troubled.

"Well then, good tidings to you and your mother until we meet again," I said in parting, as I did every day, waving to the two smiling faces before heading for the usual steep path with my black-furred friend.

"Happiness won't cooome, wandering my way sooo!"

"Meow meow!"

"It'll be summer vacation soon. What're you gonna do?"

"Meow."

"Well, you're awfully carefree. I want to go to the pool. I have a new friend now. I should try to find a pool that lets in animals as well as humans."

"Meow..."

She gave me an awkward look. She probably wasn't so fond of the water.

"It'll be fine. I can't swim a whole twenty-five meters yet either. And if you really don't want to go, I'll find somewhere else for the three of us. Life is like summer vacation."

"Meow."

"You can do whateeeever you want! So you gotta find something awesome... That one might be a little too easy, huh?"

As we chatted, we soon arrived at Granny's house. As always, I looked at the paper posted on the door, and as always I stepped inside. It was still hushed inside the wooden house, and although we couldn't hear a sound, there was no need to go searching for Granny.

These days, she was always sleeping. Sometimes she noticed when I came in, other times she slept right through. I never tried to wake her. I would sit on the floor reading a book, or look at the picture on the wall, or play with my little friend. Sometimes she woke up before I had to go home; sometimes she didn't. When she didn't wake up, I always tore a page from my notebook and wrote her a note to say we had come.

"You seem to get sleepy a lot in summer. I always get sleepy in spring."

"When you get older, time seems to go more quickly. Perhaps I'm already in next spring," she said once.

I thought it was a truly curious and wonderful sentiment. If time moved faster for you, then you could have so many more fun times in a year, after all. Even so, I began to worry about just how much she seemed to be napping.

Ever since Skank-san disappeared, Granny always seemed to be sleeping, and often times did not even notice I was there. I worried that if she napped that often during the day, she might not be able to sleep at night. But that was not all that worried me.

Summer vacation would soon be upon us, and so would the final presentation of our unit. What was happiness? The days flew by, and I could not formulate an answer. At this rate, I really was going to run out of time.

Granny was asleep again today. Sitting beside her, I stared up at the ceiling, my arms folded. But no answer came falling down from the sky. Probably because the ceiling was in the way.

Time plods on and never seems to return. No matter how much you need it, no matter how much you beg it, it never comes back. Both Minami-san and Skank-san had told me that, and I knew that they would not try to trick me, but it was only when I experienced it for myself that I realized how true it was.

Before I knew it, the day before the presentation was upon us, and I still had no answer to the question.

I had talked a lot with Kiriyuu-kun and Hitomi-sensei about happiness, and yet I'd still had no luck assembling the jigsaw puzzle of the answer. Kiriyuu-kun always seemed a little embarrassed whenever we talked about it, but at least he had decided to make his presentation about his drawing after all.

"What about you?" he asked, but I still had not prepared an answer.

"When you're drawing people's faces," he told me. "You start with a circle, then divide it in half up and down and then the eyes come next, right in the middle."

"When you're playing Othello," I told him. "You want to try to capture the corners as often as possible. Then you can't get cornered yourself, get it?"

Then Miss Bobtail and I headed off to Granny's house, like always.

Maybe I don't even need to bother heading there today, I thought, but elected to go after all.

Why would I even consider not going to Granny's house? I always went there, but for the past week, I hadn't been able to speak to her even once. She had been asleep every time I got there, not awakened once when I arrived. She just lay there on her bed, breathing softly. She was sleeping so often she might even be forgetting to eat. She seemed to be growing thinner.

If she is just going to be sleeping peacefully again today, I thought, *then maybe I am better off staying with Kiriyuu-kun and discussing happiness.* But I chose to go anyway. There was no particular reason. I had already gotten my final hint from Granny, who had lived far, far longer than me. My black-furred friend seemed to support the decision to relocate, although she probably just wasn't fond of Kiriyuu-kun.

So I headed towards the big wooden house, expecting to be stuck there thinking about how nice it would be if Granny was awake, but when my little friend and I entered the house and headed to Granny's bedroom, I was surprised to see her awake and sitting up. I let out a small "Wah!" upon seeing her. She looked my way, wrinkles deepening with a smile.

"I'm sorry, Nacchan. I got all your letters."

"No, it's totally fine. You aren't sleepy today?"

"I'm all right today. I've already gotten plenty of sleep already. And also..." she stopped, then said something that I did not understand. "I know that this is the last day."

Whenever you don't understand something, it's best to ask. "Last day for what?"

"You told me that your class presentation is tomorrow, didn't you? So today is the last day you'll have time to prepare."

"Oh yeah, that's true. That's why I came here today, to talk to you."

She smiled again. She really did seem to have grown a bit thinner.

"Of course. We can talk about whatever you like."

"Even dieting tips?"

Her laughter was the same as ever: quiet, kind, and warm. It had a different power from Minami-san's, Skank-san's, and of course my own. I was sure I would be able to laugh like that someday, once I had led a long and happy life. I felt like learning the secret of that laughter was the final answer I was seeking.

"I've got something to ask, Granny."

"Hm? What's that?"

"I want to know what your life was like."

I sat down on the end of her bed. Although it was softer than my own bed, for some reason it was also bouncier. It made me want to bounce up and down on it, but I had asked her a serious question, so I refrained.

I'm sure that Miss Bobtail was interested in hearing Granny's tale as well. She leapt up with her small and supple body and curled up on Granny's lap, looking up with golden eyes. What a truly devilish woman she was. Her eyes seemed to beguile Granny into thinking of times long past. When Granny began to speak, however, the answer she gave was a little different from what I wished to hear.

"From the time I was a child, until I grew into an adult, and then into the old Granny you see, I lived my life doing my favorite things, and spending time with my favorite people."

"Isn't that normal...?"

It felt like a bit of an anticlimax.

"Yes, that's a normal life. I was able to live a completely normal, happy life." Her voice sounded as though it was full to bursting. Full of joy. "You know, it could've happened to me, too."

"What could have?"

"Not having any friends."

All I could do was tilt my head in confusion, but Granny nodded as though praising me.

"I might not have gotten to be anyone's ally. I might not have been loved, and I might have hurt people. But I achieved it. I was an ally to the people who mattered to me. I love my friends and family. I might have hurt someone now and then, but I tried to be a good person. And so, my life was a happy one. And yet, it could have been different." She looked straight into my eyes. "I could have failed to make apologies, lost people, and be left all alone to hurt myself."

I thought of Minami-san.

She gripped my hand, which was thrust out on the bed.

"I could have self-destructed, hating myself and, worse still, tried to end my own life."

I remembered Skank-san's hand.

"But I didn't. I was able to walk the path of happiness. If I were to count out the terrible things that happened along that road, the list would never end, but there were countless more fun and happy times."

"Life is...a road?" I asked, curious about the way she talked about walking the path of happiness, and remembering the words that Minami-san and Skank-san had used.

You can't get time back. So life was like a road that ran only one way, perhaps. However, Granny shook her head.

"No, life isn't a road. There are no traffic signals in life, after all."

I giggled at her little joke and offered one of my own. "So, life is like a freeway?"

"Maybe."

It was the first time I had heard such a blunt response from her. I laughed.

"My life really was a happy one. Nacchan, are you happy right now?"

I didn't even have to think. "Yes, I have a lot of happiness right now."

I thought about my mother and father, and myself. I got to eat things I liked for dinner. I had a friend I could play Othello with. When I went to school, I had a teacher who was my ally. I had kind and wonderful Granny. I had a little friend who could sing with me. I knew I would see Minami-san and Skank-san again someday. There were bad things, too, but as far as I was concerned, there were far more happy things.

"You're clever, Nacchan, so I'm sure you understand exactly how you obtained that happiness."

"…"

"I did the same. And, I'm sure that the ones you call Skank-san and Minami-san will be able to do so from now on, all thanks to you."

"…"

"Everyone has chosen…" she said.

I felt like I could see the light at the end of the tunnel.

"To be happy."

As I finally stepped out of that hopelessly long, dark tunnel, a blindingly brilliant light exploded before me and with it, a beautiful and sprawling scene. There was the wind and uncountable greenery. There was bliss and kismet unbounded. I took a single step into that world ahead, and I felt my heart overflow with sweetness. Granny's words sent my heart soaring into flights of fancy. It was a fantasy, but it wasn't a lie. It was what I had realized, deep down.

"Thank you, Granny," I said, from the bottom of my heart. "I'm glad I came to see you today."

"Did you find your answer?"

"Yes."

It was a mystery. There were ever so many mysteries, and now I stood on the threshold of another. I was in Granny's room, sitting on her bed, Miss Bobtail and Granny beside me. Nothing about the world had changed, and yet it seemed to shine with a different light.

Granny stroked my hair with her slender fingers, as though she knew everything. Knew that my world had just shifted.

"My life overflowed with happiness, just like yours. In fact, I couldn't think of one happy thing I have not had. And yet, even at the very end, God smiled upon me. I could not have lived a happier life."

"What did God give you?"

"The gift of meeting you."

An immense happiness welled up inside of me. I had gotten to be part of Granny's happiness. I had made her happy. And I knew that nothing she had said was a lie.

"I need nothing else," she said. "The final piece in my Othello match is the happiness called Nacchan."

"So life isn't a road, it's an Othello game?"

She shook her head again.

"No, that's not it," she said sleepily, as though the pleasant, gentle light had cast a spell on her.

I picked my friend up from her lap, and Granny lay down on her side. Her eyes were only just open.

"Thank you, Nacchan," she said. "Could you open the window?"

I reached out to the other side of the bed and slid open one of the panes. A sweetly scented breeze wafted through.

"Is there anything else you'd like me to do?" I asked.

"No, that'll do...thank you."

"I'll head home then, so you can take your nap. Thank you for everything, Granny."

"Of course. I hope your presentation goes well."

She closed her eyes peacefully and I moved to leave the bedroom, my little furry friend in my arms. But just as I opened the glass door, I heard her call my name again.

"One last thing," she said. "I have something to tell you."

"What's that?"

"Listen now. Life is like..."

There was no question whether copying my catchphrase was meant to be amusing. Still, hearing her words filled my heart with more joy than the most clever joke.

I left her room, walked down the quiet hallway, donned my shoes, and stepped outside. There, I saw the grassy clearing we always came through. And yet, it seemed to sparkle with a light I had never seen before. It was all thanks to Granny. I knew that I would not be coming back tomorrow.

"Well, better get home and write everything down for the presentation."

I descended the wooden steps outside and stepped down into the grass. Then, as always, I began my song.

"Happiness won't cooome, wandering my way, sooo!"

"Meow."

The little voice that came from behind me was not one of song. I turned around at her peculiar tone. She had something important to say.

"What's up?"

As I looked back, I saw that Miss Bobtail was still sitting before the great door of Granny's great wooden house, staring at me with golden eyes.

"Meow..."

She would stay at Granny's house, she said. This was the first time that we had parted anywhere but in front of my home.

"I understand. I'll see you tomorrow, then. Try not to bother Granny."

"Meow."

Her voice sounded strange. It sounded like *Thank you,* and *Goodbye.* I was sure that this was only possible in her voice, that it could not come from human lips. It worried me, but then again, a wicked girl like her always sounded like she was suggesting something, so I waved and headed down the hill.

It was the wind that made me turn around.

A strong blast of wind blew against my body. As if I was being pulled by the wind's own hands, I turned around to face Granny's home. Or rather, where Granny's home had been.

I knew that when people were taken by shock, they never made a sound.

Before me was an empty field. There was grass, there were flowers, and there were trees. And there was nothing else.

There was no trace of the wooden house that had just been there, nor the friend I had just been speaking to.

That strong wind did not blow again.

The atmosphere in the classroom was as tense as the strings on my father's guitar. It was clear that everyone in the room—save for Hitomi-sensei—was nervous. Kiriyuu-kun and I were both nervous, despite there being fewer people to observe us this time. Far fewer than on observation day.

Our nervousness was only natural. I had spent every day mulling things over for this moment, in clever ways and ways that were less so.

As always, we gave our greetings. As always, we talked briefly about unrelated things. Then, unlike always, it was time for our final presentations.

They started with the boy in the first row on the leftmost side of the room. I could have easily ignored everyone else's presentations, focusing on reading my own over again, wondering if there was a better presentation I could give. But instead, I chose to listen earnestly to what my classmates had to say. After all, I would be sad if they didn't listen to me, what with all the thought I had put into it.

We're all different, but we're all the same.

Maybe there is just one person with an answer close to mine, I thought excitedly, but there did not seem to be any such thing. The presentations proceeded on and on, and finally it rolled around to Kiriyuu.

I was nervous, but when I looked at him, I saw that Kiriyuu-kun was even more so. For some reason, seeing the sweat beading on his forehead relieved some of my own tension. Maybe he sucked it right out of me.

I felt much calmer, and knew it was time to give Kiriyuu-kun encouragement. After all, he had kindly washed all my tension away. And yet, when I called out to him, he did not seem to hear. Instead, I gripped his hand below the desk, out of sight. He looked surprised, but when he saw my face, he bit down on his trembling lip and grinned. Slowly, his trembling vanished as well.

When his turn came, he stood and proudly—no, that might be overstating it; his voice was still very quiet—talked about his happiness.

It seemed like people still made fun of him sometimes, even after that presentation—about his drawings and, for some reason, about me. What an idiotic thing, to make fun of two people for being allies. If it kept happening to Kiriyuu-kun, and if he wanted me to, I would happily fight for him again. But I didn't fight much after that. Little by little, Kiriyuu seemed to get better at talking back, or running away.

His presentation was wonderful in every respect: whether it came to his drawing, his family, Hitomi-sensei, or a certain seat neighbor.

And then it was over, and I was next. I stood as my name was called. Suddenly, they were back: the nerves that I thought had vanished, crawling noisily up my back like worms. Again and again, I failed to pick my notebook up from my desk, my hands trembling. The notes were written in my own hand, but suddenly I could not read them. What was I supposed to do?

A single bead of sweat rolled down my forehead and someone gripped my hand, hanging at my side.

It was Kiriyuu-kun. I felt those worms suddenly retreat. I looked right at Hitomi-sensei, raising my notebook in both hands. Then I faced the class, and gave the answer that I had been thinking about for so long.

"My happiness is..."

All the way through the presentation, I remembered. I remembered Minami-san and Skank-san, Granny and Miss Bobtail, and the days I spent with all of them.

Perhaps I realized that I would never see them again.

I'm sure that I was crying.

After school that day, I headed to the faculty room. Kiriyuu-kun, who was now my usual companion on the walk home, waited for me. There was something I needed to ask Hitomi-sensei.

When I entered the room, Hitomi-sensei was talking happily with her neighbor, Shintarou-sensei. The moment she noticed me, she smiled. I approached her, saying that there was a long conversation I needed to have. Hearing this, she led me into a small, empty classroom.

Her kindness was a balm, and I was able to say what I needed to.

"I used to have some friends."

She tilted her head, and I began to speak. I told her about Skank-san, and Minami-san, and Granny, and the little girl with the golden eyes. I told her about the kinds of conversations we had, the sort of things that had happened, how they helped me, everything. *Now,* I thought, *for the first time, she might truly understand what I am trying to ask.*

"I don't understand why my friends disappeared. It's a mystery."

Perhaps this was a problem that even she did not understand. That was how mysterious these happenings were. They should have been impossible without the involvement of some sorcerer's wand. So I was shocked to see her hold up her finger like always. *That is an adult for you,* I thought. *A teacher, no less.*

Yet, in the end, Hitomi-sensei could be nothing more than my sweet, beloved Hitomi-sensei.

"Maybe they came here just to meet you?"

She was always off the mark.

"That's not true. I always went to see them."

She did not seem troubled by this response. Instead, she gave an airy laugh.

Let's think about mysteries.

With that secret lesson shared just between the two of us, we left the empty classroom. Hitomi-sensei headed back to the faculty room, while I went to find Kiriyuu. I found him in the library waiting for me. He was reading the book I had previously recommended, *The Adventures of Tom Sawyer.*

Kiriyuu-kun.

I tried to call out to him. Quietly, so as not to startle him. But my mouth and my larynx were already gone.

I could no longer speak, and finally I realized that my left eye and my right were seeing two different scenes.

That was when I realized it.

Ah, this is the end.

Chapter 11

I HAD THAT SAME DREAM AGAIN.

The short chirp of my alarm clock. The trickle of light forcing its way around the edges of the curtain. The silky sheets. The fluffy pillow. The white ceiling.

That was the first thing I thought upon waking: *I had that same dream again.*

I blinked the sleep from my eyes, moving to shut off the alarm. I felt a modest weight atop my stomach, and lifted the freeloader who always prevented me from turning over in bed, placing her down on the floor. She was such a sleepyhead that she might not wake up even if the house was on fire, so it was okay to be a little rough with her.

I climbed out of bed and stood up, opening the curtains and letting sunlight flood in. Yep, clear skies again today. Perfect weather.

Might as well wash my face, I thought, when the cellphone sitting on the table beside my bed began to vibrate. I already knew who the text was from.

As I read the message, my back straightened. I had plans for today, so I would have to get ready and go out a little earlier than usual.

I went to the sink to wash my face. My long hair kept my bedhead to a minimum, but also kept me in the bathroom longer than most. Plus, I'd had that dream today. On those days, I always ended up staring at my own face in the mirror for a while.

Once I'd fixed my hair and wrapped up my time as a temporary narcissist, I went to the kitchen and took out some orange juice and the financiers I had bought yesterday. Two of my favorite things.

It was always around this time, when I sat on the sofa to eat my breakfast, that my resident freeloader decided to wake up. She wrapped herself languidly around my legs and began licking my feet. She was probably hungry. I would be doomed if she nibbled my feet off, so I brought her personal saucer and some milk for her breakfast. I had found this saucer for her especially, one with her name written on the rim. I don't know what she was thinking as we ate breakfast, but I was thinking about dreams.

I often dreamt about my childhood, always my elementary school days. I had plenty of other important memories, but I only seemed to dream about then.

It was as if my heart was asking: *Did you do it? Did you figure out how to be happy?*

I was not suited to morning coffee, so I sipped another glass of orange juice and flicked on the TV, flipping through the channels, wondering what was on. But all I found was some old cartoons, some sad news story, and some kind of talk show comprised entirely of elementary schoolers. The important-looking college professors on one channel were saying the exact same sorts of things they were saying fifteen years ago.

I turned off the TV, leaving the little one by my feet as I moved to my office. I had lived in this two-bedroom apartment for three years now. When I searched for a home and told the real estate agent my number one requirement, they gave me a curious look. But they searched hard, and I was quite taken with the home they found on my behalf.

I had not a single unnecessary item in my workspace. I had a rolling chair beside a large desk, a notebook and pencil, an alarm clock, and a small computer. There were books on the bookshelf. And there was a blanket, upon which my tiny freeloader could sleep.

I sat down in my chair and opened up the notebook, reviewing yesterday's work. Then I took up my pencil and set to work. This job required no commute. There were no set hours, nor overtime, no coming in late or calling out early. There were no other materials I needed. My notebook, my pencil, and my mind were the only things necessary in this world.

I set the clock. Once I got into my work, I quickly lost track of time. Sure enough, the hands flew swiftly today and, as usual, I was startled back into the world by my alarm. I marked a small circle in the notebook and stood from my chair. Normally, I would just disregard lunch entirely and keep on working, but not today. Today, I had something important to do.

I fixed my hair in the bathroom, side-eyeing my freeloader, who had gone back to sleep. I dabbed on a casual looking coat of makeup, changing into a skirt that was a little more stylish and whimsical than usual. I put on my favorite backpack, and I was ready to leave.

"Meow."

The freeloader seemed to have woken. She sat by my feet, crinkling her brow and looking at me.

"What? Are you saying I shouldn't wear a backpack to a date? Listen, life is like a backpack, after all."

"Meow."

"You stand a little taller when you've got something on your back. Plus, it reminds me of a school bag. I love it."

She did not seem to understand my joke. She seemed more interested in hurrying outside, and began scratching at the door. Although she mooched off me, she always spent her days out-doors. I don't know where she went. Perhaps she was climbing hills with some little girl somewhere.

Urged on by my freeloader, I decided to leave the house at once, although it was a bit early. I had a half-read book in my backpack, a pen, and a notebook. All the preparations necessary for a wonderful time. My hair and skirt swayed in such a way that it felt like I was dancing. It would be summer soon.

"Oh, March!" I called after my cold-hearted freeloader as she left, not even waiting for me to lock the door.

She turned back with a flirty glance. I wondered what memories lay behind those alluring eyes, the eyes of someone who lived half her life like a stray. As curious as I was, it was a question she would never answer.

"I'll be back before midnight. Find somewhere to amuse yourself."

"Meow."

There was no need to worry about her, she seemed to say, bounding off on light feet, her long tail swaying back and forth. Although she looked a bit different, her behavior reminded me very much of a wicked girl I once knew.

Now then, time for me to go.

"Happiness won't cooome, wandering my way, sooo thaaat's why I set ooout to find it todaaay!"

I stretched, taking in the scenery, and took my first step out into the day.

Happiness is something that you have to choose of your own volition, through your own words and actions, by letting yourself feel joy and excitement, by cherishing the people important to you, and cherishing yourself.

I had that same dream again. Whenever I had that dream, I always felt as though my own heart was asking: *Are you happy right now?*

Whenever I had to answer that question, I made sure that my principles of happiness had not changed, then puffed out my chest and nodded.

When I was a child, a sharp young girl who always said arrogant things, I was unable to think of the people around me, and I had no friends or allies. But luckily, that little girl had people to guide her and, thanks to them, she was able to grow up.

I still remembered those people who guided me.

Skank-san. Minami-san. Granny.

Bit by bit, I came to learn the meaning of the word "skank," and the kind of job she likely had. That Minami-san wasn't really "Minami-san." That there was a plane crash on the day of my class observation. What Granny meant when she said I had the power to see the future.

They had all come to save me. And I, a little girl, was able to save them in return. That was probably why we met.

As I grew older, I understood the truth behind all those mysteries, but I wasn't sad. I still loved all of those women, and that was why I made the choices that I had. I wanted to be like Minami-san, so I used a notebook for my work even now. I wanted to be like Skank-san, so I moved into a building painted the same color. I wanted to be like Granny, so I practiced making sweets. But I still couldn't do magic.

In the end, I was never able to meet those women again.

I didn't know if I could become as wonderful as any of them, but lately my face, which once looked just like Minami-san's, had started to resemble Skank-san's. I was sure that, some decades from now, it would come to look like Granny's.

But my life belonged only to me. I could choose my own happiness.

Happiness wasn't something bestowed upon you from without. It came from within. You chose it and created it with your own hands.

I had that same dream again. Whenever I had that dream, I always felt as though my heart was asking: *Are you happy right now?*

When it came time to answer that question, I always remembered Granny's final words:

Life is something that belongs to you right now, while everything shines with hope.

I set a chair down beside him in the studio, in a spot that would not interfere with his work.

"I'm just signing it," he said, laughing at how close I was sitting.

I laughed and replied, "I had that same dream again."

I had never explained the dream to him, but he did not question it. With his pen in hand, he marked the lower righthand corner with his signature. It was something he had started using in junior high. A phrase that meant the opposite of how his own name might sound to a foreigner's ears—Kiriyuu, "Kill You"—something which might give them a fright.

"This one's for the exhibit, isn't it?" I asked.

"No," he said, looking at the drawing of rapeseed flowers in full bloom. "This one is for you."

This was his version of a proposal, I knew. *Isn't it a bit soon for this? We only just became lovers,* I thought, but I knew that he had packed all the feelings we shared into this painting. However, when it came to such important things, I preferred to hear it in words.

"Coward," I said.

He laughed and said the words properly.

How did I respond to his proposal?

What became of us since that day, even now still sitting at each other's side, is strictly under the rose.

I had that
same
Dream
again

At Night, I Become a Monster

Special Preview

NOVEL AVAILABLE NOW FROM SEVEN SEAS

© YORU SUMINO 2016

Tuesday NIGHT

IT COMES ON SUDDENLY in the dead of night when I'm all alone in my room. It comes whether I'm sleeping or sitting or standing or squatting. It starts from my fingertips, or my navel, or sometimes my mouth.

That night, the black droplets came as tears spilling from my eyes. Mote by mote, a river of unending pitch-black tears, the streams growing gradually until they fell like two waterfalls from my eyes. The simmering, writhing black drops spread to cover my face and then flowed down my neck to my chest, arms, and waist—until every last inch of my body was covered, down to the tips of my fingers.

All colors but black drained from the surface of my body at that point. I've never had a chance to watch my body's transformation, so I have no idea what it looks like. I merely get a sense of my body *changing.* Assimilating into the black drops, into a form without skin, without flesh, without bone, a form which is no doubt dreadful to look upon. But like I said, I haven't actually *seen* it, so I couldn't actually say for certain. For all I know, maybe I look rather endearing to an outsider, like one of the soot sprites from that one movie. A *makkuro kurosuke*.

When I was finally able to see my own body, it had transformed into something like a six-legged beast made of pure darkness. As I gazed at my reflection in the full-length mirror, the only things that shone on my wavering black form were the whites of my eight eyes, set above a bottomless, inky crevice of a mouth.

The first night that I viewed my own form, the black drops on the surface of my body went wild with the shock. I nearly ended up demolishing my room. However, I found that I accepted it with unexpected ease once I tried thinking of myself as something like a monster appearing in a video game or the strange beasts that I had seen in anime. How lucky that I was born in the modern age.

When I first transformed, my body was around the size of a large dog. If I want to grow larger, I can will the black drops to move and become as large as a mountain. There was no point in enlarging myself now, though. I was still stuck in my room.

I thought then that I might go outside. Careful not to smash my window the way I did on that very first night, I sprang up lightly and squeezed myself through a tiny crack in the windowsill, slipping out of my second-story room.

My body briefly scattered like a liquid, reforming into a more aerodynamic shape as I tore through the air. In a flash, I landed soundlessly upon the ground. I was in an empty lot about three hundred meters from my home. Previously, I'd just jumped as hard and as far as I could, but after landing on a doghouse in a stranger's yard and crushing it, I decided to start aiming for more open areas. Luckily, the poor pup happened to be sleeping outside his home that time. I slipped him a bit of jerky later.

The night breeze felt good, and there was a comfortable quiet around me as I expanded my body to about three times its original size, under the gaze of a half-sleeping stray cat nearby. After testing out a variety of sizes, I had determined that this one was the most comfortable for sitting, which was the closest I could get to a comfortable resting position. Seeing this dark monster suddenly spring up beside it, the sleepy-looking stray skittered away at top speed. Sorry to have disturbed your peaceful sleep, kitty.

Now a beast as wide as a road, I strode down the empty street, my six legs moving in an insectoid rhythm. Normally, this was when I would start thinking about what I wanted to do next, but tonight I had only one destination in mind.

As I continued walking, scaring off a dog who was harassing a cat along the way, I came to a crossroads. Last night, I'd turned left here and made my way out to the sea. The shore was quiet this late, and the sound of the waves put a pleasant stop to the pulsing motion of my inky form. I still had a bit of time, so I thought perhaps I could stop by the sea again tonight before moving on to my objective.

As I let the fond memories of the night before overtake me, a scream came from off to my left. I shuddered and turned to look.

I saw a fellow who had been riding briskly along on his bicycle. He seemed to have noticed my presence just as he was about to collide with me. He let out a loud scream and toppled over on the spot. I felt badly for the poor guy, but there was nothing that I could do for him. For now, I put thoughts of the sea aside and made a break down the road in the opposite direction. Whenever I caught wind of others around, I always ran away. That guy would almost certainly think that this was all just a dream when he woke up the next morning. Of course, it wasn't a dream at all. I would still be here, the window still broken, and the doghouse still destroyed.

My quick retreat was perhaps a bit *too* speedy. Before I knew it, I ended up somewhere that I didn't recognize. Hoping to get a better grasp of where I was, I moved to a nearby park and made myself larger than a house. As I swept my gaze around, far taller than even the power poles, I found that I really had traveled an incredible distance. Far on the horizon, I could see the shore where I had spent those fleeting moments the night before.

I needed to get back home before dawn. So, for the time being, I shrunk back down until I was around the width of the road again and began leisurely making my way back towards the sea.

If I ever was discovered, the ones who found me would definitely be shocked. However, it was easy to avoid being seen. For example, if I were to see a car coming, I could just leap up high enough to pass over the car unseen. Of course, I don't really have to avoid cars. It wasn't as if I would die if one hit me, and even if it did, I could simply let them pass right through me by diffusing the black drops of my body at the point of impact. The real reason I avoided them was to prevent any accidents caused by startled drivers. Besides, I had tired of the game of frightening people long ago.

Tonight, I leapt high enough to overtake any approaching vehicles. Even with a form like this, I could feel the evening breeze. I could hear sirens wailing faintly in the distance. Night is such a peaceful time.

When I arrived at the shore, I found the lovely, familiar reflection of the moon upon the ocean.

This night, however, someone had arrived here before me. Two people sat upon the beach, their arms around each other's shoulders. I got the feeling that they had come hoping to spend a little time enjoying the ocean as well. Though they were some distance away, having a monster appear at a time like this would definitely spoil the mood. I was sad to go, but I decided to quietly leave the shore behind. I was rather proud of myself for managing to be so considerate.

Seemed I had no choice but to head straight for my objective.

From where I stood, my intended destination would take about ten minutes to reach by bike. If I were to run in this form, it would not even take ten seconds. That said, I had less and less of a reason to rush now, so I took my time heading there, so as not to startle anyone.

In the end, it took me about twenty minutes to arrive at my destination. Separated from the residences and surrounded by greenery, the place was utterly silent. I stretched my back up, literally, and peeked over the outer walls. Naturally, no one was there. Melting and dispersing my body, I slipped through a tiny hole in the wall and crept into the schoolyard.

Just a few hours prior, I had been in the bath. It was not some sort of whim that led me to return to campus, nor was I interested in causing mischief. I definitely hadn't come back because I sincerely adored the school that I attended. It was because there was a change in tomorrow's schedule, and I had left my homework in my locker.

I gathered up the black drops and reformed my monstrous body. I could see glimpses of light from inside the school building, likely a security guard making the rounds. I had to be sure not to startle him, and that meant staying out of sight.

I shrank myself down a bit, pretending to be a large dog. I hugged the edges of the schoolyard as I walked towards the building. Of course, I could pretend all I want, but if anyone got close, they would see my jagged mouth and eight eyes, my six legs and my four tails, and probably have a heart attack. Even if I could change my size, or momentarily alter my form, I seemed to be beholden to some guideline that required I maintain this basic appearance—a guideline set by whom, I don't know.

When I arrived at the closer of the two school buildings, I clung to the wall, climbing to the roof in one swift move. Hoping to make a silent entrance, I hopped clear over the chain-link fence and landed soundlessly. Honestly, I should have just slipped in through one of the windows along the way, but I hoped to take a bit of a detour.

I hadn't been up on the roof since I first toured the school as a new student. I let myself indulge in a sense of loftiness, of being above it all. The illusion was slightly marred when I happened to spot a cigarette butt on the ground nearby. For better or worse, my eyes are sharp even in the dark of night.

Once I finished relishing the feeling of the wind—and my own sense of satisfaction—I slipped in through the keyhole in the heavy door.

It was silent inside—or rather, there was a low sound, some kind of electric hum. Probably a ventilation fan or something. It wasn't pitch-black, either. The emergency lamps and the light of the moon filled the halls with a dim glow.

Still, even with the sound and the light, the school was kind of eerie at night.

If I were to bump into anyone, they would be the one most surprised. Plus, I can make myself enormous at a moment's notice if need be, so I wouldn't have any trouble even if a ghost or something popped out. All the same, I felt a chill down my back. Time to hurry up and do what I came to do and get out of here.

The school building had five floors, and the third year classroom that I was assigned to was on the third. As I slowly descended the stairs, even my black drops seemed somehow uneasy, jittering silently on the surface. I passed by the fourth floor, which held the library and the art room. The moonlight piercing through the window shone upon my dark form. There was a full moon tonight.

Though I transformed every night, I couldn't help but wonder if it would be less disruptive to my life if I only transformed into a monster during the full moon, like a werewolf or something. As I arrived at the third floor, thinking about such frivolous things, I heard the sound of running water from the bathroom right beside the staircase and immediately leapt to hide myself. Of course, it was probably just an automated cleaning system. I'm not sure what I was thinking, really, given that I never looked particularly intimidating in this form.

Step by step, I approached the classroom. Class Two—my class. As I passed by a pair of other classrooms, I felt the chambers of my heart seize. I'm not sure a heart even beat within my chest, but I felt it all the same.

The end of this infiltration—which seemed strangely long given how little time had actually passed—was now in sight. I slipped in through the crack under the door at the back of the classroom. As I entered, I felt like I had been plunged into a completely different world. It was so quiet I could feel my ears ringing.

Whoever was on cleanup duty that day was sloppy, so the rows of desks were misaligned. However, it was not my responsibility to be concerned about such things, so I quickly opened my locker with one of my tails. I hated looking inside—I intentionally messed the contents up a bit, despite my daytime self's love of order.

Inside were my math textbook, workbooks, and handouts. I kept them all in line with my tail, which I could easily control. I thought through my next steps. I would have to open up the door of the classroom and put these outside before I left, since unlike me, they were too thick to pass through the small crack beneath the door. Would exiting from the hall side be less work, or maybe the window side facing the courtyard? I definitely couldn't just drop them out from the window. Perhaps it would be better to place the bundle of materials up on the roof and then come back down later to close the window? What a bother.

I scratched my head with my tail, rather than my hands, as I always did when I was lost in thought.

Then my gaze flitted back towards the blackboard.

"What are you...do...ing?"

I had been sure I was alone.

Before me, I saw the form of a girl standing with her hands on the lectern. I was so startled by her appearance that my breath stopped. I couldn't form a single word. Instead, the sensation of goosebumps rippled across my whole body. The black drops began to writhe.

As the drops trembled, they kicked up a wind and then a storm. Papers tore from the wall. Desks went crashing to the floor. The droplets continued to rage, covering the whole classroom, even reaching out for the girl and the lectern.

"Aah!"

The cowering girl's scream finally quelled the storm within my heart. The droplets ceased their rampage, and though they still seemed a bit distraught, they slowly started to return to my body. Despite their return, they refused to settle into their typical state. My whole body swelled, pulsing with violent, quivering waves.

The girl stared at me, as though she had only just barely worked up the courage to speak. I met her eyes with two of my eight. *Why? Just how on Earth? Here? At a time like this?*

I'm sure that she had a lot of questions about me, but I had just as many about her.

We stared at each other in silence.

I still hadn't forgotten that I meant to escape—I was merely concerned. I didn't know whether she had seen me fiddling with the lockers, nor if she had spotted the textbook lying at my feet, nor what I ought to do if she had.

She had me completely off balance.

"Y-y-y-y-y-you scared...me."

She suddenly began to tremble, as though in delayed shock. Or perhaps she was a little slow on the uptake and had previously set her shock aside.

The girl looked around suspiciously, eyes roving the room, shoulders swaying from side to side. She appeared to be trying to determine just what position she'd been put into. I watched her, unsure of what to do. I don't know whether she came to some silent conclusion, but she turned towards me and held out both hands, palms out flat.

"W-wait... Wait a...mi...mi...minute..."

She hurried out of the classroom. Apparently, the front door was already unlocked.

I took a brief look behind me and resolved to put the girl's reason for being here and the meaning of her actions aside. I frantically gathered up my textbook bundle and shut my locker.

Once I had hidden the evidence of my identity, a number of thoughts began to run through my head. Why was she here at a time like this, and where had she gone? And moreover, how was it that she could even bring herself to speak to a monster?

Honestly, I should have just run away while my head was still racked with confusion, leaving those questions unanswered. But I began to worry about whether she'd been caught by the school nightguard.

And so I waited.

Relatively soon after, she returned, a satisfied grin upon her face.

"I'm baaack. I went and...explained everything, so...it's fine... now."

Explained? I began to ask but abruptly stopped myself. I had no idea how my voice sounded to other people. If it was the same as normal, she might end up realizing who I was. I needed to avoid that possibility.

With that thought in mind, I should have dodged the question, but I began to wonder. How *did* my voice sound when I was a monster? Both she and I were soon to learn the answer to that question.

"So...any...way, what were you...doing?"

I did not reply.

"You're...Acchi-kun, aren't you?"

"Huh?"

A strange voice came out of my unsuccessfully stopped-up mouth. There it was.

A cold sweat—or so it felt; who knows whether or not sweat was actually there—ran along my whole body. The pulsing waves that I had been trying to suppress grew again in magnitude.

How'd she know it was me?

I glanced behind me. She had seen my locker after all, hadn't she?

"Oh, your voice...does...sound like Acchi-kun's."

She clapped her hands together very deliberately. The fact that it was the middle of the night, and that she was standing in front of a monster, didn't stop her nearly irritating theatrics.

I did not reply. Instead, I tried raising a bit of a growl, thinking that I might be able to force her conclusion back out of her head. I knew that I could howl, at least. I'd done it before to chase away a stray dog.

She tilted her head, and I thought for a moment that she might be having second thoughts about me.

"Are you...hun...gry?"

Nope. Still speaking in that strange rhythm, punctuated in a peculiar way that made it difficult to follow, she approached me until she stood just before my eyes, her feet tapping across the floor. She peered into my face. I tried to back away, forgetting my own immense size, but I was trapped.

What could I do? I should have run away at once. However, if I were to leave now, and she tried to tell others that she'd met me as a monster in the middle of the night... Well, even if no one believed her, it would eliminate the distance that I had previously kept between us. That was no good.

She could probably tell that I was shaken. A vapid smile of self-satisfaction spread across her face.

"Aaah...well."

I maintained silence.

"If you try...to pretend you aren't...Acchi-kun...then I...might have to start...spreading rumors."

"Wai—! Ah, no, uh—!"

I inadvertently let my voice return to normal as I bristled at her threat. Her smile widened, as though perhaps she was pleased to have heard my voice.

"It's...fiiine."

What was fine?

"I won't...t-tell...anyone!"

I had no idea what was supposed to be reassuring about those wholly untrustworthy words.

"And in re...turn, you can't...tell anyone that I was...here. O...kie dokie?"

I was a little startled at her proposition.

Bargaining terms. I'd thought she was some kind of idiot, someone who couldn't read the situation. Apparently, I was wrong.

She stared at me with her great big eyes.

I had lost.

After thinking on it, I nodded. I figured it was better to agree to a bargain where both sides could blackmail the other, rather than leave myself open to uncertainty, not knowing what might happen next. It was far too dangerous to let her run loose—this girl who knew the me behind the monster. She was the kind of person who always said more than she needed to.

Thinking about it afterwards, perhaps I *wanted* someone to know that I could turn into a monster. Some part of me probably wanted to take pride in it.

I steeled myself, taking care that my voice would not betray me. "All right," I said—and as I did, the girl once again gave that smile.

"Won...der...ful," she replied.

I wasn't sure I agreed. What would have been most wonderful was not getting caught by that girl at all.

...Right. Speaking of. What *was* this girl doing sneaking into school in the middle of the night? As I worried over whether or not to interrogate her, she spoke first. A peculiar question crossed her lips.

"Acchi-kun, is that...a...kigurumi?"

I swiftly dodged as she reached her arms out, trying to touch my front legs. I was unsure what might happen if a person touched me. Would anyone else really dare to touch me so suddenly? Who could imagine this form of mine to be a *costume*?

"It's not."

"Ah... I see. So...it isn't. It doesn't seem like you're...wearing a kigurumi...right now."

Though I tried to speak with a threatening edge to my voice, this girl was not one to be so easily intimidated. Once again, she tried to touch me. What was with her? She was such a...

Actually, what was with all the "Acchi-kun, Acchi-kun?"

"I don't recall you ever calling me 'Acchi' before."

In attempting to speak normally, caught up in the flow of the conversation, I inadvertently outed myself as "Acchi" out loud. However, this girl was already someone who spoke to a monster as though it were her normal classmate. She deliberately shook her head, like such small details did not concern her.

"I have...not. But that's what...you're called, isn't it? I am...
Yano Satsuki, don't...you remember? Do you like to...use nick-
names? Or...normal names?"

"...Full names. Yano-san, what are you doing here? In this
classroom?"

"I came...to play. But this is...out of hand. Let's...fix this."

Without awaiting my reply, Yano-san began to right the desks
that I had knocked over. I couldn't just stand there and watch her
fix the mess that I had made, so I began to straighten the desks
one by one with my tail. "How...convenient," she said, softly.

After rearranging the desks more neatly than they had been
when I arrived and fixing the timetables back to the wall, she
looked at me and then made a gesture as though wiping sweat
from her brow.

"Thanks...for the help."

"No big."

We had never once been together in any group or student
council or club. I felt no comfortable sense of accomplishment
from working with this girl. I'd never even desired to speak to
her before now.

Yano-san pounded her fist once. "That's...right."

I wasn't sure what she was going to say, but I got the sense that
something strange was going to come out of her mouth again.
However, it was an unexpectedly straightforward question.

"You were ques...tioning me...but before that...I'm so curious
to know, if that's... not a kigu...rumi, then how is it you look...like
that, Acchi...kun?"

I had no idea what to tell her, but I thought that I better at least say something and opened my mouth to speak. Just then, suddenly, a familiar sound rang throughout the classroom.

I must be sensitive to sounds, because I recoiled in shock.

I had no idea that the school bells chimed even at night. Though there were a few homes around the campus. You'd think that it would be considered a disturbance of the peace.

When I looked at Yano-san, however, she did not appear surprised at all. This must not have been the first time that she snuck into the school if she knew that the bells would chime. However, things were a little more complicated than that.

"Ah... Looks like...midnight break is...coming to an...end."

She pulled her phone from her pocket and fiddled with it, and the chiming stopped.

"Wh-what was that noise?"

"That was...the warning bell. If I...don't hear the...chime, I'll... forget. Midnight...break will be over in ten...minutes."

What on earth was "midnight break?" Just as I began to fume over Yano-san talking nonsense on top of her strange actions, she held both of her palms out towards me. Perhaps she couldn't tell how disgruntled I was underneath my dark, monstrous face.

"Let's...continue this...tomorrow."

"T-tomorrow?"

Did she mean during school? No way. Absolutely, positively not. There was no way I would be seen speaking to Yano-san, let alone risk looking chummy with her.

"Um, Yano-san..."

"It's...fiiine! I don't mean during...the day. Try and come here...a little earlier...tomorrow night."

"Here?"

"Yes...here. Can you...come?"

Though Yano-san didn't say it, the threat was implied that if I did not come, she would start telling everyone. The effect of her holding that fact over me was immediate. Though we ostensibly had a mutual agreement, if that agreement was broken, the damage would fall disproportionately on my side.

Having no other choice, I nodded.

What an utter, tremendous turn this night had taken, that despite this monstrous form of mine, I should be ordered around by such a weird girl.

Annoyed at the look of joy on Yano-san's face, I slipped through a tiny crack in the window and leapt outside without another word.

It wasn't until the sun was rising and my human form returned that I realized I had forgotten my homework.

My entire evening had been an utter waste.